Men—bad men—were chasing them down a mountain.

There was no place to hide. Nowhere to escape.

What did Nick do? He kissed her.

Beth was in his arms and her lips were smooth against his. She restored something in him that had been missing this past year. He lifted his head, unable to help the smile that spread across his face.

She looked up and behind them, steadying herself with her hands on his shoulders. "We should probably get..."

"Moving. Right. You going to be okay?" he asked, really curious if the near fall had bothered her as much as the thought of losing her had bothered him.

Small rocks skittered past their heads. "Great. More than great. Let's go while we can."

Choosing a path was hard. He could hear the grumbles about being caught off guard, about not doing her job, not protecting her asset.

"Am I your *asset*?"

"Of course you are."

"Beth, I've told you this before—I can look after myself."

And just like it had been scripted, he heard the lone shot of a gun and zipped back to the cliff wall, covering Beth's body.

THE CATTLEMAN

ANGI MORGAN

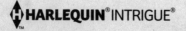

Thanks to Ron, the best cowboy I know.
Jaxon, you keep chasing those cows for your
new Pops! Jan & Robin, you are my rocks!
Can't do this without you gals.

ISBN-13: 978-0-373-69815-8

The Cattleman

Copyright © 2015 by Angela Platt

Recycling programs
for this product may
not exist in your area.

Printed in U.S.A.

www.Harlequin.com

Angi Morgan writes Harlequin Intrigue novels "where honor and danger collide with love." She combines actual Texas settings with characters who are in realistic and dangerous situations. Angi and her husband live in north Texas, with only the four-legged "kids" left in the house to interrupt her writing. They recently began volunteering for a local Labrador retriever foster program. Visit her website, angimorgan.com, or hang out with her on Facebook.

Books by Angi Morgan
Harlequin Intrigue

Visit the Author Profile page at Harlequin.com for more titles.

CAST OF CHARACTERS

Nick Burke—Owner of the Rocking B Ranch, a staging area for drug- and gunrunners. He believes there's a cartel informant on his ranch and is determined to uncover who it is while protecting his ranch at any cost.

Beth Conrad—The DEA agent who was sent from Chicago to be a member of the joint West Texas task force tracking drug- and gunrunners. But without any riding or tracking skills, it seems her fate is doomed to failure. Unless she can convince a certain rancher to help her learn.

Juliet and Alan Burke—Nick's mother and father who live on the Rocking B and are concerned for their son's health.

Cord McCrea—Texas Ranger and ranch owner, head of the newly formed West Texas task force.

Pete Morrison—Sheriff of Presidio County, Texas, and member of the joint West Texas task force.

Honey and Peach—Sisters who dispatch for the Presidio County Sheriff's Department.

Patrice—A woman who delivers messages for the drug- and gunrunners.

Mr. Bishop—A gunrunner who plays chess and uses innocents to fulfill his obligations.

Prologue

The gun barrel burned against his right temple after being fired during the attack. Nick Burke had made a fatal mistake putting his trust in anyone. A greenhorn like Beth Conrad was his second mistake. He didn't struggle, dropped his rifle to the ground, raised his hands to his ears and watched his captor kick his favorite weapon over the cliff.

He cringed as it whacked its way to the bottom of the ravine. "That was my best rifle."

"You won't need it, buddy." Keeping the gun in place, the man frisked the small of Nick's back.

He had no distinguishing accent. Nick hadn't caught a close-up glimpse of their attackers until now. If this guy was helping the Mexican cartel from the US side of the border, he was the first solid lead they had come across in a year.

Where the hell is Beth? If the DEA Agent had fallen off her horse again, he might do something crazy. Or might just end up dead. What if she was hurt or worse?

Neither was his first choice of scenarios.

"So what's the plan?" he asked, attempting to be casual. In his opinion, he pulled off not caring pretty well. He practiced it every day.

"You in a big hurry to die?"

"Been there. Recovery's harder."

"Got that right." A bit of southern poked its way through that long *i*.

"So you've been shot before?"

"Shut it, this ain't no social hour." The guy shifted his feet, stabbing Nick's temple with each move. "You listen up. You're gonna take me to your horse and give me directions out of this forsaken place. Understand? Or I'm going to kill you."

The cooling cylinder was shoved harder against his skull. Nick could feel the man's nasally breath on his neck each time he turned. Searching for who? Nick's partner or his own? He and Beth had followed at least two horses from the drug traffickers' camp they'd stumbled upon. And the cloud of dust he'd seen farther up the ravine was probably his captor's partner.

"Can't help you, so we might as well get this over with." Nick kept his eyes open, surveying as much as possible without moving. Still no Beth. "What are you waiting on?"

"Might be waiting on his partner." Beth's steady voice came from in front of them, somewhere off the trail. "But that's not going to happen."

"Get in front of me with your hands up or this guy's brains spatter on the rocks." The man shifted nervously behind him.

"Are you a mind reader? That is exactly what I was about to instruct you to do." Half of Beth's tall frame stepped onto the path, the other—the half that held her handgun—was still covered by a juniper tree. She stretched her neck, dipping her chin to look over the top of her sunglasses.

Nick had seen her do that before, just before she fired her weapon to prove how good she was with a gun. She actually could shoot the tip off a cactus from fifty feet.

He'd told her she should be in a Wild West show with that accuracy. That was if she could ride a horse. He'd never seen anyone as petrified of the animals as her.

"Do I have to officially say it?" Beth stepped fully onto the path, presenting her gun and badge. "DEA. You're under arrest. Drop your weapon, drop to your knees and cross your ankles."

"I don't get on my knees for any sweetmeat."

"That's too bad." She took a step forward.

Nick noticed the tiny frustrating clinch in Beth's jaw. "Wait. Don't shoot him. We need this guy alive."

The barrel slid from his temple just as Beth released her badge and took a very practiced stance to pull the trigger. Nick tried to knock his captor out of the line of fire, but out of the three rapid shots, at least one hit its target.

The sound of a bullet piercing human flesh was close to what it sounded like when an animal had to be put down. The sound of a man in pain was unique and easily recognizable. Both momentarily pierced his ears.

"You okay, Nick?" Beth held her gun on her prisoner, kicking the man's weapon from his fingers. "I didn't hit you, did I?"

"No. You hit him. Bad from the looks of it."

Nick rolled him to his back. A burst of red spread across the man's tan shirt, like he'd been hit by a paintball. The thin streak of blood trailing from the corner of his mouth changed the paintball image into something all too real. Nick tried to find a pulse with no luck, then searched for an ID. Nothing.

"Is he dead?" Beth asked, still standing instead of checking the man out for herself.

Nick stood and nodded, battling with himself over just how angry he was about to get. "This was a mistake. I should never have agreed to lead you back up here. That was the first guy who could give us information about the operation on my land. He wanted out of here. He would have gone for a deal. You didn't have to kill him."

"You don't know if he would have given up anything worth trading on." She holstered her weapon and put her arms around Nick. Almost as tall as he was, she dropped her forehead heavily on his shoulder. "Besides, I was aiming for his leg. He fell into the shot."

His captor hadn't fallen into the shot. Nick had pushed him into the line of fire. Their lead was gone because Nick had tried to save him. But Beth had shot him.

"I watched his partner leave in a hurry with the second horse," she said into his shirt. "He had a gun to your head. I had to shoot. I couldn't risk you getting hurt."

She was being awful clingy for a federal agent. Even one he'd slept with. He held on to her arms wondering if she would lose it after killing someone.

"He wouldn't have killed me," he answered. "I was his ticket off this mountain."

"I can't really argue about this now, Nick. Any chance you've still got your horse or any cell reception?"

"Both. The horse is secure and I can probably climb up the ridge for a signal." She stepped back, turning and stumbling a little. "Those damn fancy shoes are going to be the reason you break your neck up here."

She retrieved her badge and straightened slowly, unsteady once on her feet. She leaned against the tree she'd hidden behind earlier, then turned to slip down its side, rough bark against her back.

"Good Lord, Beth! You're shot."

"That makes sense. I figured something was wrong since I'm about to lose my breakfast and can't stand up anymore."

He ripped her sleeve, and used the ends to pad the wound in her arm. "It doesn't look too bad. Can you walk?"

"Sure. Let's get out of here before his buddy decides to make a U-turn." She pulled herself upright using his arm, then smiled at him. "Yeah, walking's okay as long as you steady me. That'll work."

Her smile flipped a switch that he thought someone had cut the electricity to a while back. Since their night under the stars, he was always crazy with desire for her. It didn't matter that they hadn't seen each other for a couple of weeks. He couldn't let her see him smile, though. He was still angry. He put his arm around her waist and started down the path to his horse.

"I realize we don't know each other that well, but are you mad at me for getting shot?"

"Hell no. Our only lead is dead." He honestly tried not to sound mad, but he didn't succeed. "Hard not to be disappointed. It's my own dang fault for letting you talk me into bringing you out here."

"Should I have let him kill you?" She pulled away and continued walking.

He admired her strength and independence, but she didn't belong here. Not in the raw mountains of West Texas. She didn't even have a pair of jeans with her. She spun to face him, continuing to walk backward in her black slacks.

"Beth, get serious. It's dangerous up here. Look where you're going."

"Well, you let me tell you something, Mr. Nick ungrateful Burke," she slurred like she was drunk, waving a finger at him. She stopped a second before he would have lunged to keep her from tumbling to the uneven ground. She swayed and he was there to catch her. "Get away. I don't need your help."

"Sure, you don't." He bent, knowing that scooping her

into his arms and carrying her to his horse was going to kill his recovering back. "Why do you think I'm ungrateful?"

"For one, you didn't say thank you when I saved your life."

"And the second?" he asked trying not to act too concerned at her swaying.

She took a deep breath and raised her finger just as her eyes rolled back in their sockets. She passed out on a long sigh and he was there, catching her before she crashed to the rocky path.

He smiled into her peaceful and gorgeous face. She couldn't hear him and it might have been the only reason he said it, but he whispered the word, "Thanks," and brushed his lips against hers.

After her inexperience almost got them killed twice, she was certain to be sent back to Chicago and out of his life. He didn't have time for distractions. He had to find the men responsible for ordering his execution.

Chapter One

Nick Burke snapped awake and heard the echo of his labored panting in his ears. The faceless man shooting him in his nightmare faded, allowing him to suck some air into his lungs. A bright beam of sun snaked through his curtains and caught him in the eye.

"What the—?" His alarm was gone. But he'd set it the night before. *Mom.* He shoved back the hair stuck to his sweaty face and scratched his damp scalp. The sheets were drenched again. "Damn nightmares."

He rubbed the numb skin covering the scars on his chest. No feeling in the daylight. Unlike at night when the dreams prodded and twisted a knife in the wound.

The more he tried to forget the shooting last year, the more he was surrounded by triggers. Literally. Stupid to believe he could face that demon and survive without some type of consequence. Cord had volunteered him to guide a drug task force through the mountains on his land and he'd met Beth. Then the shootout two weeks ago had almost gotten him shot a second time. He could still hear the bullet buzzing by his ear like a jet-propelled mosquito.

As a result, the nightmares had intensified.

He wouldn't be that stupid again. Let the task force get some other dumb rancher to help. He needed to work his cattle and prepare for winter. He'd done his part and wasted enough time chasing an enemy that would never be gone. It was a fact of life he had to get past.

Living this close to the Mexican border, it didn't matter if it was the nineteenth or twenty-first century. Cattle rustlers or gunrunners. There would always be some sort of threat out of the control of the ranch owners.

Doing everything possible to make the Rocking B successful should be his number one priority. He didn't have the time to be distracted by the task force or nightmares… or a beautiful pair of legs.

Almost a year since he'd been shot and there were only two instances when his dreams hadn't attacked him. A night of sedated dreams in the hospital while recovering, and one night in the arms of a raven-haired seductress.

The first thought of Beth started his blood pumping faster. The second thought cooled his heels in a blink. Having law enforcement constantly searching his property was bad enough. Undercover DEA was worse. Getting involved with her was out of the question. Her skill set would never be adequate for the Davis Mountains.

Sure, she could handle a gun. She'd proved that by dropping the drug dealer jamming a .45 to his head. But she was afraid of horses, for crying out loud. He was a rancher. He rode horses. Needed horses. Couldn't live without horses.

But he could definitely live without Beth setting foot on his ranch again.

A timid knock on the door had him jumping into the mud-caked jeans he'd dropped on the floor next to the bed.

"Nick? You awake?" His mother's voice was so soft it wouldn't have been heard if he hadn't been awake.

He found his digital clock across the room. Nine in the morning? "Mom, did you move the alarm again?"

"Oh, good, dear, you're awake. Are you dressed?"

He hauled a T-shirt over his head just before she pushed

the door open a crack. "Go ahead and come in and confirm my total lack of privacy as a thirty-year-old man. I've told you before that you've got to stop turning off the alarm."

His mom stood with one fist on a hip and one finger pointed in the air to halt his speech. Easier just to let her have her say. "Dear, there's someone here to see you, and I didn't want you riding off to rope a cow or check a fence."

Almost twenty-five years on the ranch and his mother still had no desire to learn what really went on here. He'd laugh, but he'd learned the hard truth of ranch work only after his foreman had shot him in the back.

"You know I'm not seeing people."

"Yes, sweetheart. I've tried a couple of times to warn you about this appointment. I even left a message on your phone."

"Appointment?"

"That's right. I tried to ask you, but since you ignored me, I've taken matters into my own hands. You'll either march into the living room or pack your bags." She drew in a deep breath and closed her eyes.

"No way. You probably have a shrink in there."

"So, you're leaving, then. Such a shame. Your father and I will miss you every day, but we'll deal with it." Her hands fell to her sides and he swore she looked three inches shorter.

"What? Mom, this is my ranch. You can't kick me off."

"Yes, it is, son, but not officially. Not yet." She stepped closer and hugged him around his waist, too short to put her arms any higher.

He patted her shoulder, thinking again. Had he really heard her correctly? He set her away from him. "You're saying I have to see whoever's in the living room or lose my inheritance?"

"We're not going to disinherit you, Nick." She turned

and sat on the corner of the bed. "Would it work if I did? Would you talk with a counselor?" She wrung the corner of her apron around her hands, obviously distressed. "How long do you think you can keep this up?"

"What? Working my own ranch? Men have been doing it for centuries."

"You know what I'm talking about. Sweetheart, you barely sleep. Don't you think your dad and I hear every time you wake up? Or creep down the hallway to watch television? Or even play those games on your laptop at all hours?" With a long sigh she sat on the edge of the bed.

"That's all normal, the doctors told you—"

She closed her eyes. She waited for him to finish. Her manners had never allowed her to talk over someone else.

"You're out the door before dawn," she continued. "And not back inside until nine or ten at night. Straight to your room and screaming from your nightmares when you do fall asleep."

"I didn't know you could hear me." His parents had never said a word. What part of his nightmares had they heard? "Do you think talking about this with a stranger is going to help?"

His quiet mother brushed a tear from her cheek. He was lost, unable to respond. It hadn't always been that way, only since…

"It's worth a try." Juliet Burke put her hands on her thighs and stood. "But that's not who's waiting for you."

Man alive, he'd almost agreed to talk to a shrink. His mother didn't know just how close he'd been to caving. He hated seeing her so concerned. Hugging her tight to his chest, he was unable—or unwilling—to look into her sad, worried eyes.

"Come on, Mom. It's getting better," he lied. He faked a smile as he released her, crossing his fingers that she'd relax and believe him for a day or two. "Does breakfast come with this meeting?"

"Of course. I was just waiting for you to get up before putting the biscuits in the oven. Beth's drinking coffee and we'll visit while you shower."

"Beth Conrad? The DEA Amazon that hates my guts? The woman who swore she'd lock me up for obstruction if I interfered in her investigation again? That Beth?"

"She doesn't hate you, sweetheart. She's come to ask a favor." His mother moved and gently shut the door as she left.

"The last favor she asked for involved me walking down a long pier and jumping head first into a dry lake."

"I heard that."

BETH CONRAD HEARD IT, TOO. She silently slipped back to the ancient fireplace in the living room as Juliet's footsteps started down the hallway. Yes, she'd been listening to a private conversation, but she didn't actually have a good track record with Nick Burke. It grated her last nerve to ask him for anything. It didn't matter that technically she wasn't the person who was asking.

"Need some more coffee?" Juliet asked, wiping her palms across the embroidered apron. The smile on her face hid any of the anxiety that had been in her voice a few moments ago.

"No, thanks. I'm fine. Or at least I am at the moment. I'm not certain how crow tastes and might choke a little once Nick is out here."

Juliet laughed.

"I don't think this is a good idea, Juliet. Your son and I haven't been the best of friends since I was transferred here. The little I've gotten to know about him suggests he won't capitulate."

"Nonsense, you don't know each other and have only met under the most stressful situations." She held up a hand and paused.

Beth had only met Juliet and Alan Burke a couple of weeks ago. After the disastrous operation in the mountains, Nick had driven Beth to the Alpine emergency room. Then he'd stuck around to give her a lift back to the bed-and-breakfast where she'd been staying. His parents had misunderstood his cryptic message and rushed to the hospital, thinking their son had been shot again. After a sigh of relief, they'd waited with their son and had insisted on taking her to dinner. Nick had fumed and protested the entire way to the café.

"Okay, I hear the shower running so we can really talk now," Juliet said. "This is beneficial for you both, Beth. We've gone all through this."

"Yes, ma'am. But just for the record, I protested then and I'm protesting now. Kate McCrea should never have twisted her husband's arm to request that I reside at the ranch. He's a Texas Ranger and technically my boss. I don't know why she asked that I be kept on the task force, I should add." If he hadn't, she'd be out of the DEA and searching for a new job.

Instead she'd act like a sitting duck. A dangling carrot they hoped to lure the perpetrator into making a move against her with. Tasked with the covert job of finding ruthless informants passing information to gunrunners and drug smugglers. Honestly, acting as bait was the only skill she felt competent in providing McCrea's task force.

And until someone nibbled the bait, they were conducting interviews and trying to covertly connect the dots.

"No one did any arm twisting. After you saved my son's life, on top of everything that's been happening in these mountains, no one had to tell me you were an agent.

Kate just confirmed what branch of the government you worked for. She's almost a member of our family. And I only assumed there was a task force involved. No one told me anything." Juliet smiled and raised her eyebrows as if asking a question.

"I'm not at liberty to discuss the investigation. I won't ever be, even if I stay here. And your family may be in danger."

"We already are, dear. This is a risk we're willing to take by staying and not selling to the corporations trying to buy us out. We just need to convince Nick that you should be here." Juliet rose, lining up the coffee pot with the sugar and creamer. "I need to get those biscuits in the oven."

"I'm completely inadequate, especially helping in the kitchen, but I'll try."

"You're not inadequate, just out of your element. Now, you wait right there for my pig-headed son," she said.

There was no way to keep from liking Nick's parents. Especially Juliet. Her husband had been very ill for quite some time, but the woman never had a bad word or complaint. Nick was her only child and suffered from PTSD after being shot last year. His state of mind was evident to everyone who knew him—and even those who didn't know him well.

One night together and she'd witnessed the tension, his avoiding sleep as long as possible, the slight shaking in his hands when others spoke of the cartel.

Juliet was at the swinging door to the kitchen. "I'm very concerned because my son was shot, nearly died and then almost killed a second time. I can't bear to think about what would have happened if you hadn't been there. We have plenty of space in this house. It makes a lot of sense for you to stay close."

Beth took a step toward the kitchen to follow.

"No, no. You stay there and enjoy your coffee. It'll be so nice having another woman around here. And you know, there really is a lot Nick can teach you."

"That's what I'm afraid of," she mumbled after her hostess went through the door.

Nick Burke had been a thorn in her side since she'd arrived in Marfa, Texas. Each way she turned in this investigation, there he stood. He was thrown in her path or she was thrown in his. Even the horrid horses she'd been on had worked against her efforts to stay away from him.

Now her supervisors had arranged for her to bunk at Burke's ranch and practically be bait wiggling on a hook. With one phone call, Ranger McCrea had assured the very people who had sent her here to fail that she had no problems. He'd told her boss that she was vital to the task force and that the firing of her weapon and subsequent death of an attempted murderer fell under his jurisdiction. The matter had been investigated and was closed.

Then he'd turned to her and said she needed to learn more about the area and enhance her riding skills.

What riding skills? She was a city girl, used to mass transit and high-rises on every corner. She'd refused to resign after her mistakes in Chicago. So as punishment, they'd sent her on an assignment she couldn't possibly complete. The wide open spaces made her feel small and inferior. Not to mention the wild animals…or the tame ones.

Nothing could be worse than banishment to West Texas for letting her guard down.

Well, it wouldn't happen again. There would be no hesitation. None. Ever.

She sipped her coffee, and wandered around the immaculate room. She lifted a picture of a young Nick and Kate McCrea back in high school. Was that a twinge of jealousy eking its way into her emotions? No. She wouldn't fall for the hurt, silent cowboy no matter how compelling his story.

But it didn't matter. She set his picture back in its spot on the writing desk. Every time he opened his mouth it was easy to push him further into a "don't touch" category. Almost as far as she seemed to have landed on his "not worth the bother" list.

The smell of baking biscuits soon filled the air. She should offer to help in the kitchen again, but she truly was hopeless there. Her mother had tried to teach her often enough, but nothing had stuck. When setting the table she could never remember which side of the plate the knife or fork should be set. Of course, that wasn't the reason she was here. The real reason was about six-three and didn't want her near him…or his mother.

"Mornin'." Nick's greeting was anything but pleasant in tone. It was something close to—but not quite—reluctant tolerance. "How's your arm?"

Beth gulped the last swallow of coffee and continued to stare out the window toward the mountains that looked close enough to touch. So did he—at least his reflection.

The T-shirt he wore was tight over a sculpted chest any woman would envy to be near. He pushed his arms through the sleeves of a second shirt that hid the uneven but nice work tan. His dark blue jeans were loose around his lean thighs. He needed new jeans to show off his perfection. She forced her body not to squirm in anticipation. She'd experienced exactly how muscular his legs were.

It was rude to keep her back to him. But as much as she'd tried to prepare herself for his arrival, facing him again was harder than she'd anticipated. At least she wasn't alone. He wasn't facing her, either.

She watched him drop his chin to his chest and rest his hands on the back of the couch that split the room from the formal dining table. It was probably a good idea to keep a large piece of furniture between them.

"Guess you're okay if you're up and about. I heard you needed a favor."

That deep voice did something to her insides every time. His sexy tone seeped somewhere down her spine and made her very aware of how his breath had touched her there—and a lot of other places. She shifted and could see his reflection in the window again, seated in the side chair now, bent at the waist, pulling his boots on. Muscles rippled in his arms just like when they'd—

Whew. She couldn't go there every time they were in the same room. But it was so easy to return to that blanket, next to the mountain fire, under a gazillion stars. His hair was wet, dripping onto his shirt. She'd seen it before. Seen just about all of him in the buff.

"That was a quick shower," she said as if she knew how long his showers were normally.

He stamped his heel into place inside his boot as he stood. "Mom's baking biscuits. Tends to get me out fast. Do you need something or not?"

All right, the biscuits were a priority and he hadn't taken a quick shower just because she was waiting. That was good to know.

"Your arm is okay. Right?" he asked with a shrug.

She looked at her sleeve as if she could see through it to the deep graze she'd received when she'd been shot. A consequential wound that had made her woozy enough not to remember exactly what had transpired before she embarrassingly passed out. "Yes. It's healing nicely."

This boring conversation was quite different from their last. At that time, Nick had said something along the lines that she was an inept agent and he never wanted to see her again. And here she was feeling like a tossed-off girlfriend. Juliet and Kate had assured her it was necessary to convince Nick that staying here was all her idea. But the women didn't know they'd slept together. That put an embarrassing spin on things.

Having to take the blame for staying at the Burke's wouldn't encourage him to believe she didn't want a relationship. Honestly, there couldn't be any fraternization now. She could fight it. She was a professional. This was her work environment. If she ever wanted to be transferred from this desolate area and back to the real action... Well, she needed to learn how to be successful here. She had to get along with Nick Burke.

Shooting the man holding him at gunpoint had been easier than facing him. He wasn't smiling. And beyond all reason she still felt the attraction throughout her entire body.

He slapped his thighs, breaking her stupor.

"So what's this favor?"

Chapter Two

"Your mother has a great sense of humor," she began, hesitating at his quizzical expression. "She, um, volunteered your ranch as a favor for the DEA. Not really a favor for me—"

She braced for a barrage of reasons why she should leave the Burke ranch. Nick couldn't possibly want her here. Should she fight him or let him win? No question, she had to fight him. This was the only place for her to learn what she needed. The Rocking B and Nick Burke were her last chance.

"She volunteered the ranch for what?" He fisted his hands and rested one on each hip, waiting for the answer. It didn't take a genius to interpret the rapid pulse visible in his neck or the dread his voice didn't disguise.

Nerves froze her in place. Even though she didn't want to watch his reaction, she couldn't turn away. "My headquarters."

"Right. That's hilarious."

"I'm not… It's not a joke, Nick. I need a place with easier, quicker deployment into the mountains."

"I'm willing to help the task force find the creeps behind the smuggling. But you don't know the first thing about a horse. How are you supposed to investigate anything?"

"That's the favor. I need you to teach me to ride and survive in the mountains."

"No way. There's no way in—"

"I'll stop you before you say something you'll regret," Juliet said, pushing through the swinging door at the end of the dining room. "Breakfast is ready. Beth, we eat in the kitchen unless we have company."

"What's she?" Nick asked.

"She's moving in. Get over it or you know the alternative." Nick's mother disappeared behind the swinging door.

He crossed the room. His boots sounded heavy on the wooden floor as he headed toward her. He didn't stop until he stood almost on top of her Jimmy Choo shoes. How he got that close without touching her, she didn't know. And she hated that if he had touched her, she would have welcomed the intimacy.

She was literally nose to nose with him in her heels. Sometimes her near six-foot height intimidated men. Not Nick. The first time they'd kissed, he'd told her how much he enjoyed the way their bodies fit. She'd enjoyed it, too, more than she wanted to admit.

Living across the hall from him is going to be seriously difficult.

Loud music filtered from the kitchen. White noise Juliet obviously supplied so Nick could have a private conversation. The woman was very smart.

"I'm not going to help you pass the time while you're here," he whispered. "On a horse or anywhere else."

"And who's asking you to?" She wanted to retreat, to give him ground. His jaw muscles clenched, his whiskey-colored eyes burned brighter with the sun in his face. She stayed put, deliberately tipping her nose a little higher. "This is business. There's nothing personal about asking to stay here."

"Good, 'cause there isn't any *personal* left between us. No matter how much my momma would prefer it that way and may push us together. You should have listened to me last week instead of concocting a reason to stay here."

"You are so full of yourself." She took a step sideways. Ready to march out the door, ready to demand another cover story and place to stay. But that was exactly what Nick wanted. "Some things are more important than our personal relationship—which I agree to be nonexistent. I listened to what you said at the sheriff's office last week. It's insulting and egotistical that you believe I'd want anything to do with you after that."

"Sure doesn't seem like you were listening. You're here, aren't you?"

"As of matter of fact, I looked for another place. But when it came down to choosing, the agency had the last say," she lied. "Since you already knew I was working undercover, it made more sense to use this as my base."

He took a step back and crossed his arms. "If that's the only reason, I'm a fly on a horse's ass."

If she said that she thought he was the rump and not the fly, he'd be even more likely to request that she leave. No matter what his mother had demanded, he'd stick by what he'd said to the sheriff and be done with investigations. How in the world was she ever going to get him to open up about the shooting? That was the only reason Juliet wanted her living at the ranch. Ultimately, Beth was supposed to get him to either talk about the trauma of being shot or get him to see a shrink.

If only her parents were here. Both were well-known psychologists and that was the reason Juliet had suggested the arrangement. The only reason. It had nothing to do with a possible romantic involvement between Nick and Beth. But she couldn't tell him that.

His strong jaw twitched with each clinch. His eyes burned into her, and she wanted to tell him the truth. Did he realize how much power he had over her when he was nice?

What if that power worked both ways? Was that what *he* was so worried about? If she were truthful about why his mother wanted her there…

"I like your parents. They're so easy to talk to. Mine dissect every word I say looking for hidden meanings. They're both psychologists."

His eyes narrowed, suspicious of her words. As he should be. "What's that got to do with anything?"

"Your parents want me to psycho-babble you while you teach me to ride."

He rubbed his old wound as he had several times when around the task force. She'd barely caught a glimpse of the scars before he'd kissed her into forgetting to look. His silence wasn't what she'd expected. First he rubbed his shoulder, then his forehead. The man was giving considerable thought to her words instead of kicking her to the curb. Or the gravel drive in this case.

"Secondhand therapy? My mom's crazy if she thinks that will work."

"I know, right?" Her acrylic nails clicked at her side and she immediately stopped them. She'd developed the bad habit after the addition of long hours spent alone, shunned by her fellow agents. She was nervous, but wouldn't allow herself to show it. "I…um…would say she's more desperate to help you. At least that's how she appears to me."

Nick's forehead had deep furrows from his concentration. "Desperate? She's desperate because of me? That's why she issued her ultimatum."

Where was the man who lost his temper at the slightest inconvenience? "It's ridiculous to think I'd be of any help. I'm not a therapist."

She could deal easier with the irate cowboy. This concerned son drew her in, encouraging her to help. Therapist or not, she knew how to deal with trauma. She'd lived it, worked through it, dealt with it daily. She probably could talk him through his nightmares. Perhaps even get him to see where therapy would be helpful. Everything she needed was bookmarked on the internet or stored on her hard drive.

Nick began pacing, looking at the ceiling, twisting bric-a-brac in circles on the mantel. "How the hell am I supposed to teach you not to fear a horse?" he mumbled, but again loud enough for anyone in the room to hear.

"Does that mean you're going to agree?" She was bewildered. Every approach she took with Nick Burke backfired.

He nodded agreement. "Dammit."

The music covering their conversation from his mother was suddenly quiet.

"Nick, please go get your father from the men's quarters," Juliet called from the kitchen, breaking up the standoff.

"Yes, ma'am," he said loud enough for his mother to hear. He marched the couple of steps across to Beth and leaned close to her ear. "Just how do you plan on explaining to the county that you're staying here?"

Just his breath darting across her earlobe made her quiver with anticipation. *Stop!* she silently cried out to her insides.

"It was suggested…" She swallowed hard, unable to state it. He'd be madder than a cross-eyed bee. Well, then, she could say it. When he was angry, it was easy not to give him the time of day. She couldn't possibly like him more than when she'd arrived here this morning. "I'll be posing as your girlfriend. Fiancée would be an even better cover. You'd be part of the team."

"You're kidding me. You want me to join their task force?"

"It's really Cord McCrea's suggestion. He's in charge of trying to find the smugglers who keep using your land. Staying here was his idea. You'll serve as the official guide or tracker…something like that. But you won't carry a gun or anything."

"The hell I won't carry a gun," he whispered emphatically. "There's no way you really think we can pull this off. We ha—don't even like each other."

He'd almost said *hate*. Her acting ability would be pushed to the ultimate limit. First pretending not to like him when they were alone. And then making him think she was only pretending to like him when they had an audience—that part wouldn't be acting. All the while she'd be secretly wanting to repeat everything they'd done on that mountain. It was so very confusing and she wasn't trying to explain it to anyone but herself.

At the end of the day, she would do what was needed in order to get away from here as fast as possible.

The stubble he'd neglected to shave beckoned to her so she'd use it against him. She reached out and let her nail scrape his cheek down to the corner of his lips. He took it, staying perfectly still, his jaw twitching even more visibly.

"Why, Nick," she said half closing her eyes and looking only at his lips. "We don't have to like each other to have fun while stuck in this situation."

His hand raised and she was prepared for him to push her away. Instead, he wrapped it softly around hers and drew the tip of her finger between his lips. His thumb drew circles on her palm and his breathing changed—or was it hers that hitched in her chest? She tugged her hand back, yet his mouth held on to its prey. She wanted to haul those lips against hers faster than a speeding bullet.

The feeling frightened her more than potentially making a fool of herself did.

Keeping cool and not reacting further was one of the hardest things she'd ever done. She could be proud of herself for not succumbing to his sexiness.

"That's the only logical thing you've said since I met you." He dropped her hand and strutted away.

The door didn't exactly slam behind him, but he didn't bother to hide the cursing as he stomped down the porch steps. Nick's feet hit the gravel on the drive and he let out a growl loud enough to be heard through the window.

"That's exactly what I said," she whispered to his retreating image.

"Did he ask about your cover story?" Juliet popped in from the kitchen and Beth had to pull her gaze away from Nick kicking a rock into the barnyard.

She nodded and faced her hostess, her body feeling the rebuff as much as her mind. "This is never going to work."

"Oh, yes, it will," Juliet answered before letting the door swing shut as she retreated into the kitchen. "I've left him no choice."

There was an extra gleam in Juliet's eyes. And for some strange reason, Beth had the feeling that she'd just been taken to the cleaners by a professional con artist.

"Staying here might well be worse than banishment."

Chapter Three

Back in Chicago, Beth began every day in the gym. No exceptions. Her trainer worked her hard and kept her body humming. But mucking stalls and moving hay bales attacked muscles she'd never known existed.

"How do you do this every day?" she asked Juliet and Alan as she creaked to a halt, leaning on the back of a kitchen chair.

"I cook, dear. The only outside muck I come into contact with is the manure for my garden."

"Speaking of which, don't you need some around your corn, honey?" Alan asked.

"Don't you even suggest this poor thing bring any to my garden. You know we don't work on it during the winter. Now, out with you, Ronald Alan Burke. Go. Shoo."

"This will tide me over until lunch." Alan patted Juliet on the bottom and scooped up a leftover breakfast biscuit with his other hand. "You've done a good job, Beth. Thanks for helping out since Nick took off to the mountains yesterday."

"Not a problem. Like you said, everybody needs to chip in."

Alan left and Beth should have followed, but she was so tired from yesterday and the couple of hours she'd worked that morning, she didn't think her feet would actually move.

"You should get cleaned up, Beth. Kate phoned and she wants you to meet her at the café. She's going to Alpine and thought you might need some things."

"Shopping? I'm not sure I can stand up long enough."

"Come on, dear. Nick can't teach you to ride in designer heels, and you can't continue to borrow his two sizes too big boots."

"You want me to buy cowboy boots? What will I ever do with them when I get home?"

"And jeans and a good sturdy coat." Juliet looked down at the extra-large overalls hanging on Beth's thin frame. "You never know when the weather's going to change."

"I have five coats back home." Beth sighed at trying to fit another overcoat into her already overstuffed tiny front hall closet.

"We're expecting the first cold front soon. Do you want to chance it?"

"No, ma'am. I'll get cleaned up."

The shower had made her feel human again, along with some serious stretching. She felt even more herself slipping into her Jimmy Choo shoes, then jumping behind the wheel. She loved driving the ranch's Jeep. The top was off, the seats faded and mud all over the body, but it was the neatest car. The cool air from outside mixed with the blasting heater at her feet. She just felt…free.

Maybe she should get something like this when she got back to Chicago. Carroll and Elizabeth would kill her. It would be impractical and get horrible gas mileage in the city. But she didn't care.

Then again, sitting in traffic she'd be choking from the other cars' exhaust. No, she'd just enjoy the fresh air while she could here in Texas.

Parking at the café/gas station, she saw Kate McCrea wave from just inside the window. Her new friend gestured for her to come inside, but didn't sit at the empty tables near the entrance. Instead, Beth followed her to the back corner booth. Cord McCrea pulled up a chair with one hand and balanced his son with the other. The remaining seat left her with her back to the door.

Exposed.

Knowing she could trust the Texas Ranger to warn her of impending danger, she sat and didn't ask to move. She couldn't complain to him or make a suggestion that he not sit with his wife. He was the boss and he'd placed himself against the wall.

In more ways than one. He was depending on her when no one else would.

Beth had only admiration for the man who'd pulled some strings to get her assigned to his three-man task force. In his shoes, she would have acted much differently. He and Kate had plenty of reasons not to want to be in the open, either. They had a long history with the cartel that included tragedy and victory over a vicious murderer just a year before. They'd divorced, remarried and now had a child. She understood exactly why he didn't expose his back to the room.

"Thanks for the invite, Kate. Juliet assured me you'd know everything I needed to get for an extended stay." She tapped her nails on the tabletop and quickly covered them with her other hand to keep them still.

"Oh, it's entirely my pleasure. Do you want some tea or something?" Kate didn't wait. She waved at Brandie and raised her own glass. "Add another iced tea to our bill, please."

"You aren't ready to leave?" Beth asked, eager to escape the peering eyes of Marfa citizens breaking for lunch.

"Believe me, I'm so ready. But we're waiting for Pete and Andrea. They're staying at the house and babysitting Danver. Cord and I have been called to Lubbock for a couple of days. We're flying there when we get back." She leaned across the table and brushed her son's full head of soft hair.

"Keep your voice down, Kate. You don't know who's going to overhear," Cord said, giving the entire room another look and landing on the mechanic leaning in the archway to the gas station.

Beth cringed at the thought of facing Andrea. The sheriff's girlfriend had no reason to trust her abilities. Her inadequacy with horses had put Andrea in danger and was yet another reason Beth needed to learn how to ride.

"I'm glad you thought about me for a shopping trip." Beth searched the occupants, too, giving the mechanic a closer look. He seemed too alert, watching his surroundings constantly. Almost like she paid attention to details and her surroundings. A well-toned body was hidden under his coveralls. He wiped his hands as if he was used to grease under his nails. Cord watched him for a couple of minutes, raised an eyebrow and the man left.

"You're the perfect excuse to take off for the afternoon," Kate continued, smiling at her husband. "Just girls. Baby and husband free for the first time in months. Cord only trusts me to be out with someone licensed to carry."

"I've got a good reason for keeping you close," the Ranger mumbled before turning to Beth. "You do have your weapon, right?"

"Yes, sir."

Kate ignored Beth's response and her husband's question, for that matter. "Shopping over the internet and in downtown Marfa's just not the same as trying on clothes. And especially picking out things for someone else."

"Where can you buy clothes here?" Beth lowered her voice so the rest of the café wouldn't think she was complaining. If her cover was going to work, she had to make them think she actually liked their small town. "The commercial part of Marfa is about the same size of one block in downtown Chicago. Comparing the two just depresses me. Sorry, I know this is your home."

"Not a problem. We know it's a culture shock for most. I attended school in Austin. Cord's originally from Dallas. Believe me, sometimes I really miss the convenience of a department store just a few minutes away."

The bell above the door rang and Andrea entered, the sheriff at her side. Kate waved and called the couple over. Beth wanted to tap "Jingle Bells" with her nails, she was so nervous.

The last time she'd seen Pete Morrison, he'd been fanatically expressing his opposition to her being kept on the task force—agreeing with everything Nick said. Of course, she hadn't been an asset rescuing Andrea from the gunrunners. She'd lost control of her horse, which had forced Nick to leave the group to rescue her.

The two couples shared pleasantries and Andrea sat next to her. While Kate invited Andrea to join them in Alpine, Beth could just nod and smile.

"Would you two want anything?" Brandie asked, handing Beth the iced tea.

"You should take the afternoon off and come with us, Brandie," she said. Then the conversation couldn't be about all her screwups.

"Sorry, I'd love to get some Christmas shopping done, but I've already sent the extra help home."

Rotten luck. Now it was inevitable that the afternoon girl talk would include men. The two women might even be bold enough to ask about her night in the mountains with

Nick. She wouldn't trade their night together, but the circumstances leading to it were consistently embarrassing.

Evade, tell the truth or lie? Three options she wasn't looking forward to. Before she could dwell on a decision, the ladies stood, handed off baby stuff—including the baby Andrea now held—and were ready to leave.

Both women knew she worked undercover and both knew she was locating herself at the ranch as bait. But she still couldn't let down her guard. She needed the shopping trip, but she needed to prove her abilities at the same time. From downtown Marfa, it was a thirty-five minute ride, straight highway with no traffic. She could keep things casual that long.

"Cord wants you to be on your toes. Both of you, of course," Kate stated once they were on the road. "Having a conversation with both law enforcement entities should clue whoever's watching exactly which side you're on, Beth. Bait the hook, so to speak."

"I figured."

"A day off from hiding while you're here in Marfa should be nice," Kate said.

"Or hiding that I prefer city life in Chicago." She couldn't forget that she didn't belong here. "My muscles are shouting with joy that they're going shopping."

"I'm done with cities. I love the stars too much," Andrea said.

Beth was having an honest conversation she couldn't afford to have at the ranch, even when she thought Juliet was the only person within earshot. The task force didn't know who supplied information to the cartel. All the workers on the Rocking B had to be treated like suspects. As did almost all the residents of the county.

"You know," she said, leaning back against the seat and stretching, "this is terrific. I'm in such a good mood.

Nothing is going to stop me from feeling great. Not even Nick's running away."

Kate and Andrea looked at her from the front seat.

Oops. She hadn't meant to be *that* relaxed this afternoon. Should she have told the task-force team while they were sitting in the café? Yes. Instead she'd shared it with their significant others just a few moments later.

"Nick ran away?" Andrea asked, laughing. "That's hilarious. Are you sure his horse wasn't frightened?"

"Andrea, don't make me referee. I haven't been out in almost a year." Kate was calm and firm.

"Okay, I'll take the one hit that I don't deserve. I told everyone up-front that I don't ride a horse, but I do apologize for missing out on all the fun that happened while I was in the mountains."

"If you're talking about all the *fun* of being abducted, you didn't miss much." Andrea was still understandably upset. "I don't know Nick very well, but I can't blame him for not wanting to get involved further. Not after being shot last year and then almost shot a second time. I don't want Pete to face any of those murderers again, but there's no way around it. He's the sheriff."

"I know Nick very well." Kate caught Beth's curious gaze in the rearview mirror. "He'll be back."

If she pretended not to have an opinion, maybe the subject would change without her admitting anything. She'd seen Nick's bravery up close. She was the reason he'd been caught and held at gunpoint. He was probably out there right now looking for signs of the cartel traveling across his land.

"Nick's okay. He's just stubborn," she finally said.

Kate lifted her wheat-blond hair off her neck. "Cord forced this on him and he's rebelling."

"From what Pete tells me, you should know. Isn't he an old boyfriend?" Andrea asked.

Boyfriend? That must be a bit awkward for Nick. And a small detail Kate and Juliet had left out of their proposition. The awkward conversation was definitely revealing.

"I've known him since we were children. Nick was never my boyfriend, no matter how much everyone believes it." Her eyes looked only into the mirror, connecting with Beth's a second time. "Should you talk about this with the guys? You can call as soon as we get to Alpine."

"His parents assured me he rides off for two or three days at a time and that he should be back tomorrow." He'd better be back tomorrow. Her agency had extended her involvement, but only for a few weeks, whether part of a task force or not.

"You can help him with that, right? Help with the running away?" Kate hinted at Nick's PTSD symptoms. "With you at the ranch, he has a reason not to run into the mountains when he's upset."

Kate looked and sounded genuinely concerned for Nick's well-being. Andrea looked confused by the conversation. And Beth found herself unable or unwilling to lie or evade.

"Well, I might actually be what he's upset about this time. He left right after I told him your idea for my cover."

"He didn't like the idea? I thought you guys were…well, you know," Kate hedged.

"Sleeping together." Andrea didn't mince words. "What was Kate's idea?"

"We're keeping it professional, thank you." Or would they? Could she keep straight when they were supposed to like each other and when they weren't? Could Nick do that?

"Seriously, what was Kate's idea?" Andrea asked again.

Ignore. She could ignore this topic. She didn't have to confirm or deny anything.

"That she's his former college girlfriend here for an extended stay," Kate answered. She looked to Beth. "I still think you need to tell Cord about this development."

"I promise if Nick's not back tomorrow, one of the hands will help me find him." Beth wished she could speak with confidence. But she had none.

"I'd pay to see you back on a horse."

"Come on, Andrea. Let it go." Kate quirked a well-shaped eyebrow that reflected in the mirror. "Finding him is easier said than done. Even I couldn't find him if he doesn't want to be found."

Kate had been born in Marfa and knew the area like the back of her hand. If she couldn't find Nick, what chance did Beth have? And Andrea was correct. There was no way she could get on a horse. But she certainly could try.

Andrea peeked around the headrest. "I'm done razzing you, Beth. I honestly wish you luck finding the smugglers in those mountains. No offense."

"Juliet said I need a new wardrobe. I hope you know where to go, Kate." Beth nodded and the subject was officially changed.

"We're headed straight there."

Beth had less certainty she could accomplish her mission. Mucking stalls and feeding animals was building her cover, but it wasn't teaching her the essentials she'd need to track down a stash of guns or drugs. She had to accomplish that in less than two weeks or she wouldn't be returning as an agent—to the Chicago office or any DEA office, for that matter.

She heard her chipped nails clicking against the hard plastic of the door and immediately clasped her hands. The nervous habit irritated her when it occurred. She absolutely hated the way they looked and felt after all the barn work. "Do either of you have a favorite salon? My nails need some help."

Andrea and Kate looked at each other and both of them said, "Okay." Did they think she was crazy for wanting nice nails? Then they giggled like teenagers and held up their polished tips.

"Call and see if Sonya can get her in this afternoon," Kate said. "You'll love her. She's the best in Alpine." Even with the thought of her nails looking their best again, her mood turned sour. It seemed there was one thing—or man—who could dampen her beautiful day. The missing Nick Burke.

Chapter Four

Nick had successfully avoided seeing Beth for two days. After the ejection ultimatum from his mother, and confirmation of it from his father, he'd taken her suitcases into the guest room. Then he'd put his gear into saddlebags and hightailed it into the mountains to look for wayward heifers.

On horseback. A sure place Beth Conrad wouldn't follow. It hadn't stopped her from calling or texting, though, so he'd shut off his phone. He'd slept under the stars to clear his head. A fat lot of good that had done him. Every time he looked up at the night sky he remembered making love to Beth. At least the nightmares had been replaced with sensual dreams.

The woman had a kiss that lasted all night long. Just the memory of it got his blood pumping. He didn't know which nightmare was worse—a faceless man with a gun or a beautiful face with a shapely body. One he'd never be able to confront and the other even living with her, he'd never confront honestly.

No matter how confusing, the open air had been good. He hadn't seen signs of any smugglers or the heifers. He'd checked all the box canyons, the cabin and had just ridden randomly to any place smugglers could be squatting on his land.

Not again. He wouldn't allow the Mexican cartel or anyone else to operate from his ranch.

That was a laugh. He couldn't monitor thousands of acres on his own. Maybe not, but he could slow them down by finding the person helping them on this side of the border. And that started by cooperating with McCrea's task force…and Beth.

He'd watched the sun rise over his land, replacing the darkness. By the time it warmed his face on the second morning, he'd come to the conclusion it was better to cooperate or capitulate. He'd thought long and hard about his parents. His dad's cancer and remission should have been enough stress for them both. Add Nick's recovery from getting shot. Yeah, that was a lot for his mom to take on.

Until Beth's arrival at the house, he hadn't thought twice about how his actions were affecting his mother. If Beth wanted to help him through a couple of nightmares, then he could talk about it for his mom's sake. If Beth wanted to fake an engagement with him, then he'd take as much as she wanted to share.

What was he fighting? The magnetism that was full-blown between them from day one? Or that McCrea had mentioned he'd been there to track smugglers not a beautiful woman?

That's exactly what he was fighting. He'd rescued her from a runaway horse instead of tracking the smugglers. She'd fallen into his arms and then into a cistern of water.

Stuck together, neither of them had held back. Then on their way home, McCrea's words echoed in his head. Had it been real attraction or defiance against a man who rubbed him the wrong way. He couldn't have a conversation with Beth without a major disagreement. They just didn't get along…except in each other's arms.

Whatever. He didn't have to agree with her in order to make his mom feel better.

His quarter horse tossed his head and whinnied. Nick reined to a stop and patted the animal's neck, keeping him quiet. He could hear movement up ahead on the trail. Which was it this time—those two-year-old heifers or drug smugglers?

He jumped to the ground, pulled his rifle and led his horse up an incline. Better to be overly cautious than dead. He'd given his word to his parents that he'd report criminal activity and not try to confront the criminals on his own.

No cell reception. Not until he reached the next ridge. He'd been out here so much he didn't need to check. Whoever was approaching, Nick was on his own. He secured the reins to a sturdy bush, got a good handhold and pulled himself to the top of a boulder.

One man dressed in an army jacket and blue ball cap was casually riding a black horse up the trail. Nick cursed and hated the circumstances that made him assume the man worked for the cartel. But if the guy didn't, he was trespassing.

Wait. Weapons. Lots of them.

No question. They were back. Probably using the same box canyon as always, moving in after he'd ridden past earlier. He was a good half day's ride from the ranch and wouldn't be able to get anyone here in time. But he'd call McCrea and keep his word to his parents.

Right after he extracted some information from the guy riding toward him.

His body tensed with anticipation, waiting. Having been shot in the back, he'd never faced his opponent. He hadn't been needed to testify. Kate's testimony had put Mac Caudwell in prison. The cartel had snuffed out his life after only a few days.

Mac had never said why he'd been ordered to pull the trigger. Nick hadn't faced him, but he faced not knowing the reason every day. It drove him to the mountains too often to look for an answer that would probably never come.

This time his opponent had a face. This time the fear wore a blue ball cap and was nearly under the boulder. Nick had jumped onto the back of a horse once when he was younger. He hadn't been able to sit comfortably for a week. It was a good twelve feet to the rocky path below.

This is gonna hurt.

He jumped, hitting the trespasser square in the shoulders and taking him to the ground. The horse bolted. The other guy took the brunt of the landing, sparing Nick's limbs, but it didn't slow either man down. He flipped to his back, sending Nick rolling, and was quickly on top of him cursing in Spanish.

"Who do you work for?" Nick grunted out between a punch to his side and a kick to his thigh. He managed to shove the attacker and scramble to his knees.

"No habla ingles," the man gritted out after Nick landed a right to his jaw.

"That's funny." They rolled, exchanging places again. "You sound more Texan than I do."

The man smiled wide, swinging and missing. Now on his back, Nick bent a leg and kicked out with his boot. He tried to stand but the man jerked him back by the collar, pulling Nick hard enough to send him headfirst over the edge of the path.

The back of his skull smashed into a rock or tree root as he alternately rolled and slid. He dragged his body to a stop in time to see the man on horseback ready to bolt, no doubt back to his *compadres*. On Nick's horse.

"See you later, *gringo*." His yellowed teeth showed lots

of ugly as he dropped Nick's cell off the cliff and left him on foot.

Nick relaxed and took some deep breaths. Not only would he have a hell of a headache, he'd also never live it down if he walked all the way back to the ranch. He'd be teased from now till he was gray and rocking on his porch. Especially by Beth.

No phone. Alone. On foot. He could still find out where the bastards were and what they had with them this time. He was a determined tracker and wouldn't give up until he found them.

Ironically, the man who'd shot him in the back and nearly killed him was the same man who had taught him how to track as a teenager. The same man who had betrayed them all and claimed he wasn't the only ranch hand working for the cartel.

Could Beth's secondhand knowledge help him learn to trust again? He doubted it. But if she could get the nightmares to stop so his mom wasn't frightened any longer, that would be enough reason to help her learn to ride a horse.

On the plus side, if Beth wanted to pretend to be romantically involved… Holding a good-looking woman in his arms wasn't a bad thing. Might be nice. Having one who knew and believed in the no-strings attached clause was even better. Hell, he could pretend to be working on his next broken heart just as much as she could.

His back was stiffer from sleeping on the hard ground than after the bullet last year. *Almost a full year.* He shook off the building dread.

The trail wasn't difficult to follow. It led straight to the canyon. He shimmied on his belly until he got to the rim, keeping hidden behind scrub. He spotted his stallion off in the far corner. And there they were.

They hadn't bothered camouflaging anything. Three

men, one wearing a blue ball cap, stood around a couple of ATVs with small satchels attached.

Money this time? Had to be since there wasn't much cargo. Money would be used to purchase guns that would be sent back to Mexico. Two men guarded an ancient-looking helicopter, rifles pointed to the edge of the cliffs, waiting and ready to open fire.

They used the helicopter to fly low through the mountains, loaded the money onto the ATVs and met up with someone else who got on the highway and away from their county as fast as possible. The rest of the distribution process wasn't complicated. They found legit citizens who still had relatives in Mexico, threaten them with harm until they bought the guns and gave them back.

Nick had done his research. It seemed an endless cycle that no one could stop. Too big to tackle. He wanted to charge down the cliff and attack. Then what? He needed his horse and wouldn't be in this situation if he'd kept his word to his parents.

He sat tight until both the ATVs started and took off. Minutes later, the chopper warmed up and did the same. Time for Nick to go.

Those men had rifles and could pick him off if they caught him in the open. He scrambled under the brush, praying his luck would improve and the chopper would head the opposite direction. When he couldn't hear the echoes any longer, he zigzagged down the path and retrieved his horse.

"At least I'm not walking, but we still have a long way to go, pal."

He didn't know how the law would get rid of any part of this operation. But he did know he had to try harder to help. There were two things he could do. The first was to get home and teach Beth to ride. The second was to have

Beth teach him to fight more effectively. He'd seen her hold her own.

He might even enjoy the close contact lessons. Who was he kidding? He'd make certain they both enjoyed those lessons. How had she put it? *We don't have to like each other to have fun with this situation.*

Exactly. It was about time he had some fun.

Chapter Five

Finally time to swallow his medicine or, in this case, face Beth. Nick knew his mom and dad were anxious and angry. They hadn't known where he'd been. He'd heard his mother's message that morning, praying that he was alive. He'd climbed to a ridge to get some cell reception, packed up, headed home and encountered the cartel.

McCrea would want to check everything in the canyon as soon as he got the news. Sad to say, but heading up there would get them nowhere. How many times had they followed that routine before? Everything would be long gone. It might be because of his run-in or maybe that had been their plan from the beginning. But they didn't know he'd seen them in the canyon.

He crossed the last fence and saw the dust trail headed for him. Two heads in the Wrangler. When they got closer he could tell Beth was driving, with one of the ranch hands holding on for dear life. She skidded to a stop, causing his horse to jerk sideways, trying to bolt.

The ranch hand jumped out, crossed himself and ran to Nick. Looked like his *medicine* would be coming a bit earlier than he'd anticipated. Off his horse, he grabbed his gear, slung his saddle bags over his shoulder and kept his rifle in his hand. A year ago that much riding would have made him too sore to move.

"Straight back to the barn with this guy, then a rub and extra oats. Thanks, Paul."

Before the shooting, Nick always sent the hands out to look for strays and broken fences. He'd stayed in the comfort of his office or had worked the horses in the corral.

"*Si, senor.* I'll take good care of him. You be careful with the she-devil. She's one crazy driver."

So, they'd given her a nickname. He had one or two himself.

"Any day now, Mr. Burke," she said, tapping the wheel.

He tossed his things into the open backseat and stood by the driver's-side door.

"Aren't you getting in?" she asked.

"Not if you're driving. My Wrangler. My keys. My turn."

"Oh, good grief." She stood, popped over to the passenger side and buckled up while he got in and did the same. "We were about to come looking for you."

"I see you bought yourself some boots."

"Yes?"

"They're purple." And had shiny rhinestones. He stifled a laugh.

"I was assured they're very popular."

He reached for the key and paused. He'd avoided this area for a while now. One of the last times he'd driven down this road had been about a year ago with Kate next to him. A different time, different thoughts, different plans for his future that hadn't been set in reality. Beth was the complete opposite, no comparison.

"You coming after me would have been fun to watch. Again. I've been wishing I had a video from the last time."

"You're hilarious."

"I needed time to get used to things." He started the engine and didn't gun it until they were well away from his horse. If he kept Beth clinging to the roll bars, she might keep quiet long enough for him to reach the hill. Or perhaps having the stuffing knocked out of her on the well-rutted, washed-out road would.

"Juliet and Alan were worried."

He knew they were and wouldn't argue. Admitting he was wrong would be hard enough to accomplish. "I'll take it up with them. You've got my curiosity up. How did you know I was headed home and why the rush to get me there?" He shouted enough to be heard over the engine and the wind rushing by their ears.

"So you didn't think we'd be coming to look for you?" she asked, looking ahead with only one hand holding to the door frame.

He skidded the Wrangler to a stop as he crested the last hill to the house. "What do you need to say to me that can't be said where I might raise my voice and blow your cover?"

Eyes as big as a baby doe's, she stared at him several seconds. "How did you figure that out?"

"I took more classes in college than just animal husbandry. But it really didn't take much to get four from that two-plus-two equation." He pushed his hands through his hair instead of reaching out for her as he wanted. They might as well get the apologies out of the way. "So what did you want to see me about?"

"We didn't really get a chance to talk much before you took off. Your mom mentioned she saw you. So I, um…I just thought it would look better if I seemed excited to greet you."

"Right. It has nothing to do with how anxious you are to hear what I found out there? And it doesn't have anything to do with whether I decided to walk away from all this or stay and help you with your cover?"

"Go ahead, drive. I'm not in any hurry to hear anything." She leaned back, trying to look casual. It didn't look good on her. He liked that she stood and sat straight. Taller than everyone in the room except for him. Casual didn't fit. "I really didn't care when you got back. You were gone three days. I can't help it if people began to wonder why you left."

"On the very day you arrived, too. Must have been hard to explain. Probably even harder to your friend McCrea. My parents get it. I leave all the time."

"Makes no difference to me. I get paid the same, whether you help or not."

She clenched her jaw just as she did when holding her opinion to herself with the task force. Her teeth might split in two if she bit down any harder.

"And what if I said I did see something in one of the box canyons. Is there still no rush?" He watched the raven-black braid fly from its casual spot across her breast to hit the Wrangler seat as she turned to face him. It was hard to hold back his laughter. He raised his eyebrows and clenched his jaw so he'd appear serious. "Want me to take the long way home?"

"Are you kidding? Why are we waiting here?" The smoldering look she returned spoke every ounce of the frustration she'd obviously experienced. "We need to get a team together and get there as fast as possible. You should have called."

He scratched the three days of beard. "I'll be glad to hit the shower and get some of this stink off me."

"Then why don't we go to the house?"

He flipped his seatbelt off his shoulder and stood in the worn seat, gesturing for her to follow. She did. He leaned forward on the windshield frame like he had many times in the past year, just looking. And wondering where the men were who had ordered his death.

"Have you taken a look at a map, Beth? Do you have any idea how long it takes to get anywhere in this country? Especially on horseback?"

"Believe me, I study area maps all the time. In between my daily chores, that is. We should get moving. There's a lot to arrange."

Agent Conrad had ranch chores? He swallowed his surprise. Who did he have to thank for that bit of pleasure? "I should have thought of assigning you duties before I left." He waved a hand in an arch toward his land. "Tell me what you see, Beth."

"A lot of nothing in that direction. The ranch is behind us. What's your point?"

"That's exactly my point." He was disappointed, but she said what he'd expected to hear. How most people reacted. "You see nothing."

"Can you stop speaking in riddles, Nick? So there's a lot of nothing between us and wherever this box canyon is. How far can we take the cars?"

She was such an attractive, competent woman. It would have been nice to imagine her here because she wanted to be. Because she saw the beauty of the land just like he did. Of course, appreciating the ranch had taken quite a while for him. He couldn't expect that reaction from anyone overnight. Or even in three weeks.

Making love to Beth had been a welcome reward for getting pulled into that cold water cistern after she'd been dumped there by her horse. He'd been looking forward to getting her onto a soft mattress once or twice before she headed back to Chicago. But that was before she'd declared herself his protector and had been assigned permanently to this idiotic task force.

She tapped the back roll bar. He remembered her long manicured nails. The vivid memory of them being dragged across his back and then barely touching the puckered bullet scar had combined both of his dreams into one.

The best and worst thing that had happened this past year.

He pointed to the highest spot in front of them. "Up there is where most of the activity's been."

The sun was setting. Still high enough to just catch the hilltops and make Nick shade his eyes.

"It was clear this morning. No signs they'd been there in a while. Then I had a fight with one who destroyed my cell and stole my horse. I tracked the horse, waited until they pulled out and came home. In the time it took me to ride down, I've seen dust clouds. Heard sounds of a second chopper."

"Let's go. Now." She popped into her seat. Out of the corner of his eye, he saw her head tilted up to him. "I *will* find these guys and put an end to the threat they pose."

"No, you won't. That's the point. In all this vastness, you can't do this alone. Not without a lot of help and manpower. You have neither. Just me and a lot of ground to cover. You think of me as just a rancher, someone to teach you the necessary skills to complete your mission so you can move on. But I live here. This is my land, my home."

"Look, I realize they twisted your arm to help me and that you might be—"

"No one can force me to do this, Beth," he interrupted before she could make him angry. Hell, she'd already made him angry. "Here's a secret, I don't live here because I have no choice. I'm not afraid. You need to stop thinking that I am or we'll never leave the paddock."

"I don't think of you that way, Nick." Shoulders back, shades on the top of her head, she implored him with her eyes alone. "I never could. If I didn't respect your skills, I wouldn't have asked for your help."

"You're asking this time instead of the DEA?"

She laughed, tossing her braid over her shoulder, making him wish those gorgeous black locks were flying free in the wind. "The DEA doesn't need to learn to ride one of those monsters you call a horse."

The sun disappeared. Staying up here would give credence to their engagement story. *If* he was going through with this charade. "I had another reason for stopping."

"It can't wait?"

"Man alive, you're just flat impatient."

"I'm efficient." The little remaining light was behind her and he couldn't see her expression. But the agent had returned, standing straight and resting her hand on her hip.

"I stopped to give you a chance to say something without my mom and dad in the room. Don't you have something to ask me?"

She jumped from the Wrangler and walked around to the hood, lightly hitting it with the palm of her hand.

"I don't think I should. You've obviously made up your mind that this is a hopeless situation and you're unwilling to help. I'll just go back to the B and B tonight."

"There you go jumping to conclusions again." He'd decided to go through with this earlier and he didn't know why he wanted to tease her so much with *what ifs* now. But it felt right. "You mentioned something about a fake engagement so everyone thinks your staying here is legit."

"Yes. Does that mean you're agreeing to teach me how to operate in this territory?"

"I wouldn't go that far. But I'll teach you what you need to get by."

"Yes." She did a classic double fist pump gesture for emphasis.

"That is if you ask me. And if I were you…" He ducked

under the roll bar to the ground. "I'd ask me real nice-like. Bended knee, the whole shebang."

"Oh, my gosh. You can't be serious. It's a *fake* engagement."

He gestured to the rocky ground again. "Not to everyone out there."

"You're for real? You want me to kneel? No one can see us. Oh, all right. Whatever." She shoved his chest, causing him to retreat a step and giving her room to bend on one knee. "Okay. So. Um, Nick Burke, will you?"

"Wait. I think you're supposed to hold my hand or something."

She rolled her eyes and grabbed his hand, sighing as if touching him was going to absolutely kill her. "Will you marry me?"

"Marry you? I don't even know you." For some unexplained reason he couldn't help teasing her.

"Okay, that's it. I'm out of here."

He squeezed her hand, keeping her where she was while he knelt in front of her. Their thighs touched. It was clear that two layers of jeans weren't enough to stop the sparks he remembered.

"Go ahead. I'm ready and will behave."

"Again?" Beth cracked her neck exactly like she did before taking aim. "Fine. Will you marry me?" she asked in one long monotone breath.

"Sure. But I want to be up-front with you. I believe in long engagements." He helped her to her feet.

"Thank heaven." She started to slip away.

Someone probably watched them through the telescope they had on the patio. That's how his mom would have known he was close. He knew it, but Beth didn't. The entire gesture thing was to make her cover story believable.

He should tell her. But not telling her for a minute was much more fun.

As many times as they'd kissed, even the first night they'd kissed, they'd never been standing. Now he held her close to his chest and slid his arms around her back.

"What the heck do you think you're do—"

He kissed her. And kissed her again before her hands went from trying to push him away to sliding around his neck. Her lips were as soft as he remembered. She tasted like fruit. Strawberry or maybe cherry.

It was hard to remember that someone, most likely both his parents, were taking turns watching. His fingers itched to drop a few inches and curve around her shapely bottom. Instead he wrapped them around her waist and explored her cool mouth.

When they came up for air, Beth's dimple was prominent in her cheek.

"Worth going down on one knee?"

"Don't get so full of yourself." She pointed a finger in his chest. "It doesn't take a genius to figure out this was for your mother's benefit. I finally remembered the telescope."

There wasn't a sharp jab from the tip of her finger. He grabbed her hand and took a closer look. "You cut your nails?"

"I realized it would be better if they were short. Easier to do ranch work. I took care of it in Alpine with Kate. I don't mind."

He did. He'd miss them. "Kate? When did you see her?"

"We went shopping. I needed appropriate clothes if I was going to take my turn mucking stalls like everybody else."

"I have hands for that. Who the hell said we took turns?"

"Great. Just great. I am going to kill your father," she said through gritted teeth as she walked back to her seat.

"Hey, Beth?" A Wrangler width's between them and he continued to feel the heat she'd created being against his body. He wanted to stay and wait for the stars to come out instead of heading toward the house. He was very tempted to ask but that wasn't the objective. "There's another reason for you to stay on the ranch besides my mom's ultimatum."

He could see her smile, her brilliantly white teeth showing in spite of the darkening sky. Time to fill her in on his adventure at the canyon.

"I'm going to find who the cartel has spying at the Rocking B. I'm ending this once and for all."

Chapter Six

"I'm telling you that they ain't doing nothing except riding. Day after day, that's it. Burke ain't going nowhere. He ain't taking off like he used to. Not even to town. And there ain't been a soul come to visit them. Nobody. That makes it too risky."

The past several weeks had been very frustrating for their organization. Their Rook had been captured, leaving only the three of them. The promised weapons had been confiscated. And this American imbecile was getting on his nerves.

"We want him out of the way. Do you understand?" he asked, expecting the appropriate response.

"No. Spell it out for me. 'Cause you don't and won't ever pay me enough to take care of that kind of a problem. Do *you* understand?"

Impertinent fool. If the organization had anyone else to take their place on the ranch, his men would chop the body in pieces for the Coahuila desert mountain lions to feed upon. They needed this little pawn, much to his distaste.

"I understand perfectly. It's a shame you do not. All we require is an opportunity to present itself."

"They ain't givin' you none."

"I have excellent hearing and I heard you earlier. Perhaps we are paying you enough to give them a false lead?

Once they're in the open, I have men who understand their jobs and can take care of the problem."

"When are you thinking? There's no way I can pull something off before tonight. But everybody's talking about what happened last year, him being shot and all."

"Tomorrow will be soon enough."

"I'll call ya."

The line disconnected.

"I'm sure you will," he said, setting the phone on the table.

As he sat on the gold brocade settee, he studied the four chess boards to his left. Each one a separate opponent. One—the Rook's board—would go unfinished. He didn't care for that scenario.

Unfinished bothered him.

As did the unfinished business of Nick Burke. He shouldn't have trusted the money-fixated foreman to take care of that particular problem last year. His personal men would have been more efficient and they might have had control over the property by now.

"Working in that area is one constant irritation after another."

"What's that, *senor*?" Michael set a dinner tray on the end table.

He'd been so deep in thought that he hadn't noticed he was no longer alone. It re-emphasized just how annoyed he was.

"Nothing, nothing. I was thinking aloud. Nothing to bother with, Michael."

"Do you need anything else this evening, Senor Obispo?"

"No, and tell the rest of the staff I do not want to be disturbed."

"Very well, *senor. Buenas noches.*" Michael gently pulled the door closed, leaving the room silent.

Perfect.

They all knew him as Senor Obispo. "Mr. Bishop." He pulled the dark wine-colored bishop from the game he'd been playing with the Rook. He would have won in four moves.

Senor Obispo could afford to bask in his victory. He rolled the cool marble between his fingers and gripped it in his palm. Mr. Bishop needed action—swift, sincere, artless. He stared at the other three boards against the wall. His opponents were merciless. He mustn't fall behind in any of the games.

The one adversary he truly wanted to outmaneuver was Burke. The game would be simplified when he did. How many moves would it finally take to defeat him? An inconsequential nobody who didn't know he was at war?

Tomorrow. His answer was patience. Tomorrow the game would change.

Chapter Seven

Hand to hand. Hip to hip. Chest to chest. Back to front. Tense muscle to tense muscle.

Beth drew in the sexy scent off Nick's shoulder pressed very near her mouth. Nice. Enticing. Erotic. Off-limits.

"No, not spread. You'll lose your balance. One foot slightly ahead."

"Like this?" His lowered voice sent tingly shivers throughout her body, teasing the cells that remembered his light but firm touch under the stars.

"Yeah." She gulped air through her mouth, trying not to smell his intoxicating musk and get turned on even more.

Another move had his rock-hard back pressed against her breasts. Her in a workout tank and him in a sleeveless undershirt only stirred the memory of when no cotton cloth had separated them. She had a stranglehold around his neck, his hand was behind her head, fingers twisted in her hair. She wasn't threatened, only proud when his free hand followed through and she was forced to release him.

The daily encounters of physical contact with Nick were probably the only things keeping Beth sane on the ranch. She was in charge, the expert. She could hear her parents drilling the phrase "knowledge is power" into her brain. They'd forced her to learn constantly. It had driven her at school, at college and at work. Not any longer.

Book smarts couldn't make up for experience.

Constantly learning about riding and horses kept her busy, but also made her feel inadequate. Where her parents were concerned, she'd never be the smartest person in the room. And here at the ranch she was once again the student. She'd never enjoyed that position. It made her feel totally vulnerable.

More so than having Nick's hands casually touch her during a lesson or when he was pretending to be her fiancé.

Nick didn't hold back while they were working out, so neither could she. He was an avid student, forcing her to teach defensive moves she'd learned from instructors years ago. They trained in a silent barn before everyone awoke. At a horrible hour before anyone should be awake.

"Your elbow should catch them a little higher." Her soft voice was to hide their secret workout. She wished she could protect herself from his knowing eyes as easily. He could tell when she was close to breaking their agreement about no sex.

He could tell and he would tease her mercilessly.

Nick raised her exhausted arms, bringing them back around his neck for another try. More pressure, a tighter hold, slick skin, more effort. A breath across her ear made her lose focus. He chuckled. She wanted this one as a win. Forearms, elbows, she pushed the exercise out of her mind and dealt with the threat.

He spread his feet. That was her opportunity and with a determination she'd thought she'd forgotten, Nick went down.

"Damn, woman." He moaned a second or two with his eyes closed. "When are you teaching me that move?" He stuck his hand blindly in the air, expecting her to help him stand as she'd done each time before.

"You didn't angle your feet." Touching him was difficult, but she did. They clasped forearms and he stood.

Face-to-face, his chest only inches away from hers. Closer than she felt comfortable allowing others. Not close enough to satisfy the desire building inside either of them. She could see his rapid pulse, caught the slight jerk when they touched and witnessed the heat in his eyes.

"Sun's coming up," she whispered, breathless and sounding wanton. "You ready for a shower?"

For a long second, she saw the invitation in his eyes. The one he purposely had teased her with all week in front of every person on the ranch. The same suggestive invite that he stealthily secured then hid behind a blank look and a shrug.

She reached for the towel she'd brought from the house, and then her feet flew over her head. Flat on her back in a pile of hay, Nick towered over her, laughing.

"My feet?"

"Spread not staggered." He winked.

Beth stayed put, waiting for the right moment to bring Nick to her side on the ground. Gone was the desire to share an intimate moment. The adrenaline pumping through her veins was about winning, about the teacher not being outshined by her pupil. "Oh, man, I don't think I can move again."

He took a step closer, lowered his hand ready to help her to her feet. She closed her eyes to keep from giving herself away. She played her feminine card, breathing harder, knowing that her chest was propelling her thinly-covered breasts closer to him. Knowing that no matter what was or wasn't between them, under it all…he was just a guy. His stance weakened as he bent to check on her and she struck.

Lightning fast she whipped her hand behind his ankle and yanked. With a resounding *whack*, he joined her on

the hay pile. The moaning next to her was a positive indi-
cation she'd succeeded in her mission.

"I'm thinking that move isn't totally fair."

She twisted her face toward his, almost as close as when
his back had pressed against her. "Why do you say that?"

"I don't have that weapon in my arsenal. Never will."
He rose on an elbow, his eyes cutting to the cleavage at
the top of her tight sports bra.

It was her turn to laugh. "No, I guess you don't."

"We should head to our respective corners before we
break something." His fingertips skimmed the top seam
of her tank.

It was worse torture than if he'd pinned her shoulders
to the ground. She couldn't move. Her pulse raced in anticipation. She craved more. Another stroke. A single kiss.
Shoot, just holding his hand when they were alone would
be nice.

"What could we…um…break out here?"

"The rules."

He rolled away and stood, leaving her to fend for herself. If he hadn't, she would have been all over him. It was
better this way. Much better. She'd be heading home in another week. Sooner if she didn't conquer her fear of those
four-legged monsters at rest in the stalls.

She'd never caught herself wishing for things to be different, but…

She really wished their situation was different.

"Meet you back here after breakfast."

"Not today." He swiped at the straw stuck to his loose
jeans.

The man really did need new clothes that fit him after
all the workouts he'd done this year to get strong. Of
course, then everyone else would see what was hidden.

Beth sort of liked the idea that she was the only woman who knew about the hidden muscles.

She swallowed hard, trying to hide her excitement. Nick might mistake it as excitement for the horse. "I thought I had to saddle Applewine all by my lonesome today."

"You do, but dad can supervise." He began walking out the door, swinging his arms into his jacket.

The weather had turned much colder in the past couple of days. She'd already mentioned to Juliet she was thankful for the thicker coat she'd purchased in Alpine.

"Wait. Why can't you walk me through it?" He was hiding something from her. "Are you driving to Fort Davis? Marfa? Abilene?" She watched him shake his head as she ran through the town names. "But you *are* going somewhere."

"I'll be back in a couple of days."

"You are not going into those mountains without me, and there's no use arguing about it."

He slammed his hand against the wall and then dropped his forehead against the painted wood. "You can't. I need to be on my own tomorrow."

Tomorrow was the anniversary of the day he'd been shot. Everybody was worried about him. Honestly, she'd expected to find him gone today instead of sparring with her. Her change of clothes and toothbrush were already in saddlebags his father had provided.

She comforted Nick—as much as she could someone in his situation—by placing her hand on his shoulder. It was his only body part she trusted herself to touch. "I'll go with you. It'll give us a chance to talk."

"It would be a lot simpler if you just let me handle this."

"We both know that's not a good idea."

He pivoted and her hand slid across his rigid chest. She recognized the angst, the worry that he'd lose it. The tick in his jaw was as pronounced as the worry wrinkle between his eyes. Gorgeous eyes that excited her with each glance. They warmed her just by looking at her, as if she'd swallowed a shot of whiskey instead of sinking into the depths of his gaze. But she had to set her attraction aside. What little advice she could give, he needed it. Soon.

He covered her hand still at the base of his throat. She could see his rapid pulse, feel the anxiety pumping with every beat of his all-American heart. His lips flattened tight with anger, his grip was the tiniest bit too tight, his eyes were narrowed slits. Whatever he was about to say would be brutal so she'd be angry. So he could leave without her.

Or at least try.

Then it was gone. He looked totally relaxed, waiting for her to overreact. Two could play that game and she was much better practiced at it than he. She'd been fooling her parents and DEA personnel for months.

"You still aren't going without me," she whispered.

"I didn't say a word." He quirked an eyebrow high and dropped her hand.

"Oh…you shouted volumes."

NICK RUBBED JUST under his shoulder. Probably out of habit instead of it hurting. He almost couldn't tell anymore. They'd been riding a couple of hours and Beth had been handling her horse well, listening to his instructions without complaint. So what was bugging him?

What wasn't bugging him?

A week ago he'd had every intention of taking Beth up on her offer to have some "fun" during her stay on the ranch. Every day the objective should have been plain. She looked more than willing, yet he went to bed alone. He liked her. The most surprising thing was that he respected the effort she put into learning ranch life.

Conversation around the dinner table flowed easily about her life in Chicago, shopping or adjusting to West Texas. She'd missed Thanksgiving with her family the week before, so his mom had made a second turkey dinner with all the trimmings. The only thing missing had been a Dallas Cowboys football game.

Not bad on the eyes. He hadn't known he liked tall women until her horse had thrown her in that water cistern. Her hair was much more than just black. The sun bounced through the strands like blue flames.

She caught him staring at her, but he didn't stop. He didn't have to.

"Why in the world do you call this poor beast Applewine? That's not even a real word," Beth asked, picking a twig from her horse's mane near her gloved hands.

"Mom wouldn't let us call her Apple Vinegar."

"Now that was just mean, wasn't it, girl?" She patted the bay's neck, then sat straight. "Your dad said we should have snow soon. Are you really planning on spending two nights out here in the open?" Beth twisted in her saddle, then stretched in the stirrups. She was clearly uncomfortable.

"You seem kind of…fidgety." Her movements made him laugh and wince at her discomfort at the same time. "I could radio for one of the men to come get you. I'm not going to get into any trouble up here on my own."

"Famous last words. How in the world do you keep… um…*things* from going numb?"

"You'll get used to it." He laughed, keeping it low so she wouldn't get mad. He'd probably laughed more in the past week than during the entire past year.

But then it hit him again, a wave of "nothing in life mattered." Whatever he did, he wouldn't stop smugglers from using his land. It was a hopeless dream to try. Maybe he should get out, sell, move. He'd thought about it many times while staring into the mountains. He'd suffocate in a city.

That was the crux of his problem.

Afraid to stay because of his unknown enemies. Afraid to leave because he'd just die a slow death making a living somewhere else.

"I could enjoy this ride a lot more if this were a cool gel saddle." She stood in her stirrups again, giving Applewine a looser rein, which encouraged the horse to trot. "Whoa, sister."

"Sit and pull back a little." Watching Beth's antics, he should be enjoying the ride a lot more.

His body grew too heavy to move. He couldn't get the image of the corral out of his head. The feeling of icy cold continued to seep into his veins no matter where he was. He could search the storm clouds building over the ridge, but the white pipe fence built itself piece by piece. The last thing he'd seen as he formed the last thought he should have while dying.

"You, um…okay?"

Beth had stopped her horse and his had stopped next to her. He hadn't noticed. He'd gotten completely lost reliving the moment he'd been shot.

"Want to talk about it? You said you would, you know."

Yeah, he'd promised. He searched the opposite horizon to avoid her concerned eyes. At the time he'd given his word, he'd meant it. This week had been okay. The nightmares had been replaced with dreams of tossing Beth into the hay—for different reasons than practicing self-defense.

"Nick?"

"Tomorrow. That's when it happened." He answered without wanting to.

"Right."

"I couldn't be there. Looking at the corral. Wondering…

Thinking it would all happen again." The slow motion fall to the frozen ground replayed in his mind. He couldn't stop it. He couldn't *not* see it. He felt his flesh tear. Felt the hot searing and ultimate pain—

"Nick!" Beth shook his shoulder.

How had she gotten so close? *Damn.* He was falling for real. Almost on top of her.

"Should we pull over for a while?"

"What?" He swallowed hard, almost choking, holding back a roar of laughter. "We don't really *pull over* our horses."

Potential anger or not, he couldn't hold it in. He laughed at her mistake so hard he bent forward over his saddle horn, rubbing Rocket's thick neck while he was there.

Beth dismounted. He couldn't see her face and would probably need to smooth over his inconsiderate treatment of her ignorance. Oh, God, he could see her shoulders shaking. She leaned into the side of her saddle, crying.

Nick swung his leg and jumped off the right side, next to Beth. He dropped an arm around her shoulder thinking of something positive to say. Anything that could make up for belittling her. "I didn't mean to laugh—"

Beth tipped her head back. There were tears leaking from the corner of her eyes. Tears of laughter. She drew in several deep breaths, slowing down to talk. "Oh, wow, that was so funny."

"I thought you were upset."

"Oh, no. Pull over a horse? Ha ha. I crack myself up." She hobbled to the edge of the path, bending at the waist and stretching.

He took the reins of both horses, enjoying the view. He liked that about her. She'd apologized while admitting she knew nothing about riding, but then laughed at herself without a second thought.

Joining her near the slippery rock slope, he stuck his

free hand in his front pocket while the other kept the horses just behind him. He tried to back up with no luck. There was plenty of open space around them, but it sure felt snug.

"We better get moving and get to high ground before this weather turns on us." If they stayed there, he'd kiss those soft luscious lips that tasted like a Chapstick version of cherry that he couldn't get enough of. Then he'd fall into her, letting every curve she had press next to him. Pulling her closer until it wasn't close enough.

"Nick? You okay?"

Stumbling backward, he startled the horses while slipping on loose pebbles under his boots. What the hell was the matter with him today? He'd practically had Beth's clothes off in his vision. He could feel the blood rushing, the anticipation of taking her was already killing him. He swiped at his sweating brow and knocked off his hat.

Applewine spooked as if a rattlesnake were striking. She reared up, pulling his arm with it.

Beth's fear didn't keep her from rushing forward, latching on to her horse's bridle and yanking down. Shoulder to shoulder with Nick again, she rubbed Applewine's light tan forehead with her knuckles.

"Don't you dare bite me, you old nag."

"I got 'em."

"Are you certain? You seem to be fading out somewhere."

The first pings of sleet bounced off his hat that had fallen to the ground. "Time for talking later. Mount up. We've got to get shelter."

"Are you sure we can't just hug a tree trunk until this passes?"

"You'd be standing there quite a while." He snatched his hat from the rocks.

"You're crazy."

"So I've been told."

"I did not mean that like you think."

"Cover your face with your scarf, keep your head down and let Applewine do her job. Just relax. She'll follow behind Rocket without questioning a thing. If you could do that, I'd appreciate it."

A quiet harrumph and her lips tightened like she'd superglued them together. She clicked and cooed to her horse as she'd been taught, but was silent for the hour it took to get to the cabin.

They stabled the horses where she opened her mouth, looked at him, and then changed her mind. Warm, brushed and fed, the animals would be protected and comfortable in the lean-to.

Maybe he should have told her about the cabin earlier and that they'd have a bed—or couch—to sleep on. But he hadn't made up his mind to head this direction until the sleet had begun.

Imagining the impossibly close quarters of a tent was what made him hightail it here.

He grabbed an armful of wood from the pile near the cabin. Beth did the same.

"What is this place? And don't you dare say it's a cabin. I can see that much."

"Then why did you ask?"

She dropped the stack of wood, then placed her fisted hands on her hips and cracked her neck as if she was about to pull a trigger.

"We actually crossed over to Kate's land. The place belongs to her, but I use it from time to time."

"So no sleeping under the stars to clear your head tonight?"

"I thought this would be a little more comfortable for you." He knelt to start the fire.

"Actually, I won't lie. I appreciate it. I could do with some hot coffee and grub."

He couldn't help it, his head whipped around to look at the city girl who had just used the word *grub*.

"Isn't that the word?"

"Sure it is, but since when do you talk like that?"

"I figured, when in Rome… Your dad says it like that all the time when he signs off from his chat rooms. I've also heard it in the movies." She'd fallen asleep watching a Western almost every night. "Where's the coffeemaker?"

"I'm building it."

She let out a long sigh and collapsed on the bench seat next to the door.

"Dinner's leftover turkey and biscuits. They're in my saddlebags." He knelt by the fireplace, stacking and breaking some homemade quick starters into the kindling.

Beth closed her eyes.

"Coffee's there, too."

"Sorry, I don't think I can move." But she did. She flipped open his gear and dug through the side with food, then shuffled her boots across the wooden floor before she plopped on the couch. Opening the ziplock bags, she dropped them on the coffee table.

He remembered all too late what he'd thrown in the top of the other bag. Condoms. How would she react if she knew he'd had no intention of leaving without her this morning?

Now that he was here, he had no intention of starting the generator for electricity. Yet. He had other ideas about how to keep warm.

"Is that a working potbellied stove?"

"They didn't haul it up here for decoration. I'll get it started after I get water on to boil."

She pulled a pillow next to her and sort of slid sideways to get her head to it. She was asleep before he could get inside a cabinet and retrieve a blanket to cover her up. He tugged one of her purple rhinestone boots and then the other, dropping each. The loud noise when they hit the floor didn't get a flinch. She was passed out like he'd slipped her a sleeping pill.

"There's always tomorrow."

He piled logs on the fire, closed up the food and toed his own boots off his feet. There was a comfortable mattress in the other room, but he'd get stiff from the cold. He took a step toward the rocker, but instead he lifted Beth's head, deciding on the end of the couch.

She squirmed a little, settling comfortably in his lap. He draped another blanket over his legs, tucked her blanket up to her chin and closed his eyes, regretting the images of Mac holding a gun and a person with no face pulling the strings.

The fire had faded and the room had chilled so he must have gotten some sleep. Beth mumbled a couple of indiscernible words.

Glancing at his watch, he saw it was after midnight. The day he'd dreaded for weeks had arrived. A day to avoid. A day to make decisions. Funny thing was…all he wanted to do was lie down next to the woman who was already halfway in his arms.

If he could hold on to her, he had a feeling that everything would be fine—at least for a little while.

Chapter Eight

Beth woke with a blast of thunder. A bolt of lightning flashed, filling the room with a blinding white light, then another loud crash. At some point, Nick had carried her to bed. She was so tired she'd slept through it. Unfortunately. She would have enjoyed his arms around her.

"You okay?" Nick asked in a whisper of a whisper, so soft she wondered if he was a dream.

So soft was his voice that if she hadn't been awake, he wouldn't have interrupted her sleep. And he wasn't interrupting it. Not from that far away in the stiff-backed chair. She'd given her word not to push a relationship, but he'd given his to take full advantage of having fun.

With all the hard work they'd been putting into learning to ride and self-defense, wasn't it time for some of that fun?

Another lightning bolt struck. The thunder followed too quickly.

"That was a little close."

"Always seems closer up here." One of his arms was crooked behind his head, supporting it. He couldn't be comfortable trying to sleep there. If he was trying to sleep at all.

Beth pushed into a sitting position, resting her back against the headboard. She was still fully clothed without her boots. "I must have been exhausted to have slept through dinner."

"And moving you here. We both fell asleep. You warm enough? I could start another fire."

The flash outside the window backlit him again. But she knew what his face looked like. She'd studied it all week and could tell when he was full of concern or teasing her by offering to do something with no real intention of following through. Their week had been full of polite comments and then a jerk of his thumb gesturing where an item was located so she'd get it herself.

He was lying about him getting any sleep. He rarely did. And she didn't care about a fire. But she wanted warmth. His warmth.

"You'll have a stiff neck in the morning if you stay like that." The bright light from the storm illuminated her watch. "Oh, gosh, it's only one o'clock? I feel like I've had ten hours of sleep."

"Snored like it, too."

"Take that back and I'll let you share this mattress with me." Great invitation. But she didn't want to take her words back or lie that she'd misspoken. She actually meant it exactly the way it sounded.

Nick rubbed the stubble on his chin. She could hear his nails scrape lightly and shivered. She knew what his chin felt like against the softness of her skin.

"I was just teasing. You don't snore." He sat forward, leaning on his knees, hidden by the darkness. "If you're cold, I guess I could keep you warm."

She began to scoot to the opposite side of the bed, but the cold sheets—even through her clothes—brought her to an abrupt stop. "You'll have to make do with me in the middle. I am not about to freeze my tush off over there. I'll never get back to sleep."

"Do you need more sleep?" He stood and pulled his tan shirt, then the black cold-weather shirt off, leaving the white undershirt in place.

"Do you?"

Memories from their night in the mountains made her fingers curl around the edge of the quilt. She kicked the covers away from her legs. Desire heating her skin made it ache for the coolness of the crisp air.

Light from the storm hung in the room long enough to see his jaw clench. "I don't think sleep's in the cards to-night."

For a second she thought he referred to making love to her. Then she understood what day it was. Of course he wouldn't be sleeping. It was the reason they'd come here. He'd been shot a year ago today.

Her body cooled in the mountain air. Then she saw Nick's belt was unbuckled. She didn't need any light to recognize the sound of a zipper slipping open or his jeans falling to the cabin floor. It wasn't as far to the bed as when he'd been sitting in the old chair. She didn't have long to wait.

She wasn't cold any longer. The thought of how they'd warm each other was pushing everything else from her mind. She shimmied out of her own jeans, leaving the un-attractive long underwear in sight.

Even unable to see Nick's features she knew he laughed slightly at the sight. She didn't care. She'd leave them on if it lightened his heart for a few minutes. Her fingers were at her waistband, ready to lift her legs awkwardly and pull them off before he took another step.

"Hold on," he whispered again.

His hands covered hers, lifting them to her sides. He gently tugged and her leggings curled down her thighs, followed by two burning trails made by his knuckles. He rolled a wool sock to her toes, rubbing her ankle, then massaging her foot. She could have died and gone to heaven right then. But her experience with Nick let her know that dying wasn't necessary… Heaven was just minutes away.

First one foot and then the other. He kneaded her sore muscles right up to her thighs. She gasped, not from embarrassment or shock… "Pure bliss. You must have a lot of practice massaging women to have honed your technique to perfection."

He laughed from his chest that time. "The horses seem to like it. Roll over. I know what's really sore."

"That's not—"

He crossed her ankles and began flipping her to her stomach. She allowed her body to follow and immediately received a deep kneading. His comfortable, knowing touch soon made her relax. And moan. Especially when he reached her back and shoulders.

"Stop tensing up."

"Are you kidding?" she mumbled into the pillow. "You'll need a bowl to scoop me into soon. I'm melting like ice cream."

"Not yet you aren't." His tone changed, both in his voice and hands.

Instead of the deep massage her muscles had wanted, his strokes were long and feather soft, feeding a different craving. He no longer touched her through her clothing. His calloused fingers skimmed across her skin exciting her entire body. He leaned over her, nuzzling the base of her neck.

Barely touching her with his lips, he then dragged the tip of his tongue to her shoulder. She wanted to squeal with delight at the way he caused her body to react.

Since he leaned on the side of the bed, she turned onto her back again. But before she relaxed, she removed her shirts. Nick helped, tossing them on the chair behind him. She began to remove her bra, but his hands delayed her action, gently pushing her shoulders to the mattress.

All the while, the storm raged outside the thick-paned window. The lightning was more rapid followed by almost constant rolling thunder.

Rugged fingertips traced the outline of the top of her bra. She might have been wearing long underwear and working on a ranch, but the black lace made her feel at home. Much more herself. Even attractive. Almost as attractive as how Nick was making her feel at that moment.

"You are so dang beautiful." He fingered an errant strand of hair from her face.

She was far from beautiful and parted her lips to protest, only to have Nick pull her quickly to him and slash his mouth across hers. She'd missed kissing him during the past two weeks. As close as their workouts had brought them, the temptation to taste him again had been there every day.

She stretched her arms around his back, wanting skin. But he was still in his undershirt. She knew he'd stay within the safety of the soft cotton to keep her from seeing his scars. No matter how much she tugged, he'd distract her by being extra generous with himself.

They fell to the soft mattress, his hard body stretched on top of hers. He ran a hand down her thigh, guiding her leg to bend and wrap around him and making her heart race at the intensity of his touch.

He traced her collarbone with his mouth. "I love your legs. Love the fit of you against me." He emphasized his words by dropping his pelvis against hers.

Her mouth opened again and his tongue was there to pleasantly invade, dancing a dance that had stood the test of time. Without words he invited her to join him.

Or maybe she'd been inviting him all along? She didn't care. She wanted him and it was evident he wanted her. She slid her arms higher along his back, under his shirt. He quickly pushed himself up, taking the pressure of his chest from hers and lifting his back out of her reach. She immediately missed his warmth, his weight…his everything.

She shoved her arms to unlock his elbows. He descended back on top of her, catching himself in a push-up at the last minute. She used his surprise to flip and roll him to his back. She pinned his shoulders, keeping his shocked, gorgeous eyes focused on her. They'd performed this move a hundred times in the hay with almost as little clothing separating their bodies.

But now…

Now they didn't have to worry about someone walking in and discovering them. Close enough to know how the next part of this journey played out. Only a couple of heartbeats from heaven again.

"That's a beginner move. You're so past that. I can't believe you let me get the best of you." She spoke softly and close to his whiskered face.

"Babe, that is definitely not the best part of me." He stretched. His mouth seized her nipple through the lace. "Come here…and I'll show…you…" Between his words he scraped his teeth gently, then captured her sensitive skin again.

What could she say? She gasped. She could only remain motionless and absorb all the wonderful sensations pulling at her body. At every smidgen of her body. Luxuriate in the tingles pooling and building like a bottle of champagne that needed to be uncorked.

How could this man affect her so deeply? Attraction was one thing. This was so much more. Did she have the same effect on him? He'd sworn he wouldn't succumb to sex, yet here they were. Had he taken her up on the fun she'd so bravely offered in retaliation to him recoiling at their fake engagement?

Why the debate? She could have fun. So much fun. And, oh, gracious, she could feel. His hands wrapped around her breasts, kneading them until her arms were wobbly and she collapsed on his chest.

His knuckle nudged her mouth to his once more then continued around to wrap his fingers at the back of her neck. He held her in place. His kiss was hard, excited, ready…along with the rest of him.

She gulped part of his air and forced her mouth away, letting the day's scruff on his chin scrape her cheek. She hooked a finger on each side of his boxers and inched them down his legs.

His large hands framed her hips, but hers stopped their exploration of his chest. He quirked an eyebrow, questioning her. "Oh, yeah, sorry. It's in my jeans."

"You certainly were sure of yourself packing a condom on your mountain campout."

He tried to move, but she remained sitting lightly across his thighs. The white of his shirt was easy to see, unlike his eyes. She was so excited she was breathing hard and way too fast. She needed to be daring, bold.

"I want to see you," she finally got out.

A bright flash filled the room. It took a moment for her eyes to adjust and when they did, he pointed to his body.

"That's about all there is." He grinned, the white of his teeth reflecting the little light from the other side of the window.

"You know what I'm talking about." She lifted the bottom of his undershirt. "You don't have to hide it. Or is there some reason you don't want me to see you completely naked?"

He threaded his fingers through hers, bringing their fists together at his navel and removing them from the edge of his shirt. "I haven't let anyone. Not since the hospital."

"Does it hurt?"

"It's not supposed to," he whispered.

She didn't understand why it was important to get his shirt off. Maybe she wanted more than just a meaningless bout of fun. But it was important. A step toward getting to know the real man and not just the guy who was part of her assignment.

A crack of thunder and shot of lightning made her jerk back, taking his hands with her. He followed. They sat awkwardly with their hands somewhat near his lap.

The moment of their passion had passed, but he hadn't said he wouldn't show his scar to her.

She slowly backed off his legs and tugged him to his feet. They might have looked silly, moving to a thick-paned window…her in black lace underwear and him wearing only a white shirt. She drew him closer to the window. The wood floor froze her feet. The cold air made her shiver.

Nick tried to pull her into his arms, but she refused. Her fingers went to the edge of his shirt as their eyes locked and she tried to be reassuring. It wasn't her best characteristic. Her parents had reminded her several times.

Seconds later, Nick raised his arms and his shirt was off. He was breathing hard, as if he'd run the Lake Michigan shoreline. She flattened her palms over his chest. Compared to hers, his was fiery hot. Warmth shot through her arms.

Touching him was enough to fuel the fire between them. He closed his eyes, one hand on the windowsill, one across her shoulder. He looked petrified. She could feel his forearm muscles tense, attempting to get himself under control.

"This isn't a good idea."

She couldn't stop. She couldn't be detoured by the desire to comfort him. This was important. Even without a proper term to describe it or a degree in counseling, she knew it was time he showed her.

Distant thunder. A gleam of distant light. More distance between them.

Keeping her eyes locked with his, her hand skimmed the light dusting of hair across his ruggedly hard chest. Again he stopped her. Was her hand trembling or was his?

"It's okay," she crooned, trying to convince them both. To convince them that everything would be fine for him and that she knew what she was doing. She dropped her gaze to the puckered, jagged scar. She gently touched the edges.

Nick threw his head back and closed his eyes, unable to watch the look he knew would be on her face. It had been bad enough with the nurses at the hospital.

Beth had a gentle touch. He wasn't worried about that. The pain was in his head, not his shoulder, not his chest. The creased skin wasn't so bad in his back. A smaller hole that hadn't torn him apart like the exit wound.

Beth's nails drew an outline around the top of the jagged marks, then came to an abrupt halt at what hardly anyone knew about. She looked at him, questioning the six-inch scar down his breastbone. Her hand flattened over his heart. She leaned forward, gently kissed his scar and rested her cheek against him.

"I died. On the table. They were trying to get the bleeding under control and my heart stopped instead. The surgeon told me he thought there was no chance." He tried to laugh it off. Tried not thinking much about those minutes that he couldn't remember. "He calls me a miracle."

"Shh." Her breath wafted lightly across his skin.

"Mom and Dad sort of know, but not the details. They… I've never shown—"

Her finger over his lips cut him off. "Shh." She laid sweet, gentle kisses the length of the six-inch line.

"I know it's not pretty. Let me put my shirt back on so you don't have—"

Beth's hands slid around the back of his neck, easily guiding his lips to hers. "You talk entirely too much. Do you know that?" She kissed him and his arms encircled her.

He totally got caught up in standing straight and kissing a woman who was nearly as tall as he was. He liked it. Liked it more every time it happened. Their tongues tangled a brief moment before Beth spun him and pushed him back on the bed.

"Where were we before I got distracted?"

He rushed to the middle of the bed, ready to heat up the cold sheets. Beth rifled through his jeans and slowly stepped out of her panties. He couldn't stop watching her, memorizing every inch of her as she straddled his thighs. His tall feminine warrior knew exactly what to do, and he was ready for her actions.

Now wasn't the time to stop things again to light a lamp, but he sure wished he had. He wanted to see every long curvy line of her, every crease in her skin, every freckle— or find out if she had freckles. He wanted to see her sexiness, the way she looked when she reached her highest peak. Wanted to recognize exactly what it was like when he pushed her over the edge.

"Come here." He pulled her to his chest, kissing her like crazy again. His hands glided across skin as soft as silk, unsnapping her bra and letting it slide down her arms between them. She pulled it free and flung it aside. Her nipples had pebbled and felt erotic against his chest.

Then their hands were everywhere. Roaming, searching and exploring in ways they hadn't taken the time to do the first night they'd been together. He wanted to know every subtle change, wanted to feel her hair—

Her hair was still in the tight braid she plaited every day. He hadn't ever seen it loose. Reaching for the end, he slid the elastic holder into his hand.

"Oh, no, no, no. It's such a mess." She grabbed the end of the braid, tossed it down her back and stretched, reaching for the stretchy loop still in his hand. "Nick, give it back please."

"You took off my shirt. I should get to see your hair."

"Can't we wait until we're on a date or something and I have time to straighten it? It'll be as curly as a Slinky."

He shook his head and shot the band across the room. He captured her surprised mouth and attacked her lips, distracting her while his fingers worked through her braided mane. He eagerly awaited the next bolt of lightning so he could see. He settled for her soft locks flowing down and teasing his shoulders. When she moved, it caressed him like a handful of silk feathers.

Beth pushed to a sitting position again, searching in the dark for the condom she'd retrieved earlier and had tossed on the covers. He caressed her slender hips, his thumbs inching their way to her intimate secrets.

She allowed him to discover how to please her and when she begged for release he hesitated, savoring the magical way she looked. Darkness seemed to shroud everything in the room, but it was the first time in years Nick felt surrounded by light.

It followed Beth wherever she was—especially now. Her eyes were soft, her breasts lush and the tip of her tongue peeked out between her lips. One last touch and she cried out her release. The first of many, he hoped.

Beth collapsed on his chest. She found and tore open the package and slipped to his side, dragging her nails and teasing him to fullness. She raised up, her hair swishing across his abs in a wavy curtain.

Nick pulled her body even with his so she rested on top of him. Slowly he threaded his hands through those curls and guided her lips to his, indulging in the scent of wildflowers in her hair.

Beth tried to move to one side, but he kept her where she was. With very little maneuvering he slid his length into her, creating a pleasant rhythm for them both. Beth kissed his chest again, then placed her palm over his heart. She sat and their rhythm increased until they climaxed beyond mere satisfaction.

With the last throes of passion still echoing through the room, Nick shifted to lie at Beth's back, tucking his arm under her pillow and pulling her cool skin close to his. He possessively cupped her breast, kissed her shoulder and skimmed his fingers across her belly.

"Storm's moving on."

She was right. The lightning flashes were fewer and farther apart. The thunder rumbled down the mountain toward Marfa. It had barely rained, but it was cold enough to ice. The trail would be hard tomorrow when they left.

If they left. There was nothing to rush back to at the ranch. It might even snow. They had plenty of food, heat and each other. What else did they need for the moment?

"I suppose you're tired." She hooked her finger on the corner of the covers and pulled them closer, waiting for their bodies to cool before pulling the comforter over them both.

"Not really." He softly dragged his fingers in circles across her hips and her legs. Man, oh, man, he loved her legs. "What did you have in mind?"

He nuzzled her neck and shoulder, tasting the light saltiness the exertion of their lovemaking had created. His hot breath penetrated the cold air of the cabin that was quickly cooling the woman in his arms.

"Actually, I need food," she said, twisting a little to get a look at him. "What about you?"

He laughed, short but deep from his core, thinking of the extra condoms in his saddlebags. It was a good beginning for the anniversary of the worst day of his life.

Chapter Nine

"Get dressed." Beth shook Nick, ignoring his moan that he hadn't slept the first half of the night. "That sounds like a car. But it can't be. Right?"

Nick bolted upright, jumping from the sagging bed. He ran to the small window and opened it five or six inches. "You're right. I hear the echo of an old truck or a couple of ATVs."

"But don't you have to come here on horseback? I mean, you admitted at breakfast that you were heading here all along yesterday, so if we could have driven…"

Nick shoved his legs through underwear, socks and jeans. He didn't look up until he was stamping his foot into a second boot. But she knew. It was a cabin that could be accessed by a car, and he'd tortured her backside just so he could get his hands on it.

"You better get dressed."

"What's wrong? Didn't you ask permission to borrow this place?"

He took her shoulders and made her face him. "Beth, no one comes here this time of year. There's no telling who's heading up that path."

"As in…the cartel."

"As in we're getting out of here before we find out."

"You're right. This position has too many blind spots

and can be breached easily. But we're not going to have much luck on horseback and might not have enough time to get them saddled."

He shoved her clothes into her hands. "Get dressed. Grab the food and saddlebags. I'll take care of the horses."

He swung into his Sherpa wool coat, shoved his hat on his head and pulled the door shut behind him. She was wasting precious time. Once dressed, she ejected her magazine to verify it was full and slipped her arm through her shoulder harness.

Five minutes and she was out the door, stamping her own boot into place while she juggled the saddlebags and her coat. How he'd saddled both horses in that amount of time, she had no idea. She ran. He secured the bags and shoved a .38 down the back of his jeans.

It was definitely ATVs. There was a roar of more than one engine, at least three, maybe four. "Andrea was abducted by men on ATVs."

"Yeah, I know." He mounted, still holding Applewine's reins. She reached up for them but he nodded to step into his saddle stirrup. "I'd pull you up, darlin', but you wore me out."

"I can't ride like that."

"We're going down a mountain as fast as this horse will take us. You're riding with me." He held her steady as she swung behind him. "Hold on and do not let go."

She heard the whoops and hollers of the men on the ATVs. They were close. "Once they get to the cabin, there'll be no doubt we were there. Do you think they'll come after us?"

"Yeah, I do. I shouldn't have brought you."

"You didn't have much of a choice."

Drawing the informant out into the open had been her primary assignment on the task force.

She clung to Nick as he left the trail, dipping when he dipped to avoid low branches, leaning backward when they hit an incline. All the while thinking she should have stayed and confronted those men. But with whom? Nick was a private citizen, not a trained agent. She couldn't put him at risk like that. But not staying had blown a perfect opportunity to prove her worth. She needed to succeed.

"Hang on, Beth, and don't scream."

The side of the mountain fell away in front of them. She couldn't see anything except gray sky as Nick leaned back in the saddle, taking her with him. The horses picked their way carefully down the steep incline of rocks and scrub. If she stuck out her hand, she'd touch the cascading rocks and debris.

Shocked beyond silence, she held on for dear life knowing if she fell she wouldn't stop falling until she hit the ravine below. The shouts and curses from the men—now many feet above them without a way to follow—echoed off the cliffs.

Minutes—that seemed like a lifetime—later, Nick clicked to his horse and headed on a trek that mountain goats would have had a hard time following. But at least they were sitting straight and not headed down anymore.

"Oh, my gosh!"

"Don't look down. Is anyone following us?"

The view to her left was a cliff, complete with no way down. She latched on to Nick's waist tighter than before and looked over her right shoulder.

Everything had happened so fast, she hadn't realized that Applewine was free and hadn't followed the way down. Rocks cascaded behind them. On a higher level, she saw a man skid to a halt, whooping when he caught her horse.

"I should have kept hold of her reins."

"Just watch." Nick clicked encouragement to Rocket.

The man put his foot in the stirrup and the entire saddle slid to one side and to the ground. Applewine was startled into following the impossible path.

"The belt thing, under her belly. You didn't tighten it." Riddle of the superfast saddle master solved.

"That's only one guy. Any direction we go they'll be able to cut us off. With the ATVs they're going to get there before us."

"We use the radio. Call for help." Thank goodness they'd packed it in Nick's saddlebags.

"I'll get us to a level spot."

She couldn't see the man or any of his friends at the top of the ridge. She'd glanced away too long and didn't know if the man who'd fallen with the saddle had gotten up. She also couldn't turn or lift her head from Nick's shoulder. Not until she knew there was actual land to look at again.

"I didn't see any of their faces. Did you?"

"They were covered with bandanas or moving too fast." Nick laced his fingers with hers across his abs. "I can feel your heart racing."

"Well, yeah. We just shot over the edge and…and… You might live this kind of adventure, but I've never done anything like that in my life."

"That was a first for me, too."

"Oh, gosh, that makes me feel so much better," she said with as much sarcasm as possible. "My parents never even let me ride roller coasters."

"I did ride one or two of them when we lived in Dallas. That cliff was just as good. Here we go." He released her hand and pried her fingers from his shirt. "We should be able to catch our breath and see if the radio's working or if anyone's listening."

They dismounted and he brought out a bottle of water

with the satellite radio she'd been issued for the task force. Beth took the radio and walked the trail behind them, searching and listening for anyone following.

Nothing.

"Will Applewine be okay? It's awful slick out here."

"Keep your fingers crossed and keep calling McCrea on that thing. I'll be right back."

"No. We should stay together."

"She's not far and I've got this." He pulled the .38 from his back. He jogged down the piecemeal trail. "I'll be right back."

Time ticked away as she spoke her radio sign over and over. She checked and rechecked the frequency. "Lordy, girl. Hold on while I get the sheriff."

Snap!

Beth turned the volume down and listened. She not only heard the sound of rocks hitting each other, she saw one or two roll across the path Nick had taken.

"Beth? You okay?"

"Pete, approximately five men are chasing us. They arrived on ATVs, haven't fired, but I'm assuming they're armed."

"Where are you?" the sheriff asked.

"Somewhere south of the Danver cabin. We're on horse-back."

"Can Nick get you to somewhere a chopper can land?"

"I don't know. He's not here and I don't think we're close to anything flat enough." Her lack of knowledge about this land was a serious handicap. "I can't see any plausible site."

"Son of a— You got separated?" Pete asked.

"Not exactly. My horse—"

"Not again. I thought he was teaching you to ride."

Believe what you want. "Stay by the radio. When he gets back, I'll have him tell you exactly where we are. Over."

Tap. Tap. Another trickle of rocks.

Nick wouldn't be playing games with her. He'd seen her shoot first and ask questions later. So either a wild animal was stalking the horse or someone had caught up and was attacking from above.

NICK CLICKED FOR APPLEWINE. He held out his hand, pretending to have sugar. She wouldn't budge from the open spot on the path. He could hear faint voices from the ridge and needed to get back to Beth.

What the hell had he been thinking taking off like this? Putting her in danger was the last thing he'd wanted. He wouldn't pretend that he'd had any real intention of coming out here on his own. Getting away from the house and the concerned looks had been the biggest reasons for an overnight. Getting Beth alone…yeah, that had been pretty high on his list, too.

He wouldn't regret last night, just his idiocy at bringing her to the cabin.

"Get over here, you old fly catcher. We might just need you to get out of this mess. If you bolt you're going to break your neck…and mine."

More voices. The bay moved in his direction.

"That's right, girl." He kept his voice low, crooning to the mare.

An ATV engine roared to a start. He jerked around in time to see a rope falling over the side of the cliff. He didn't recognize the man. One thing he knew, none of them were there to help Beth.

Damn!

Applewine nudged his shoulder. He grabbed a handful of mane and pulled himself up onto her back. Reins in one hand, his .38 in the other, he stayed low against her neck, hoping his coat would blend in with hers from a distance.

Surefooted, the horse followed the makeshift path on her own while Nick watched a man lower himself over the cliff. Rushing the horse on the cliff side was impossible riding bareback. He couldn't call out to Beth and warn her. He'd soon be at a point on the path where they could take him out with a rifle.

All he could do was pray.

Hooves connected on rock for an irregular clip. He could run for the spruce tree he'd left Beth under. It was less than a hundred yards away. The man would shimmy down the rope faster than Nick could run, much faster than the horse would clop.

A movement below him showed someone at the bottom of the ravine. No way the ATV guys could already be on their way back up. He slid off the mare, ready to make a run for it, then he saw the reflection. What little sunlight through the clouds there was bounced off a black halo of hair.

Beth hadn't had time to braid or pull her thick mane into a ponytail. It hung free, just below her shoulders, just below the boulder at his feet.

"Nick. Nick." She waved to get his attention. "We've got company."

"I've seen them. Did you get in touch with McCrea?"

"The sheriff needs a location for a chopper to land."

There wasn't any ridge close. He pulled the bridle off Applewine, slapped her on her behind and sent her down the path so she'd be safe. Joining Beth, they picked their way back to the trees. But there was no way out.

Her mouth fell open when he unsaddled Rocket and let him loose to join the mare. He shrugged. "There's no other way."

"There are lots of other ways. The first would be discussing it *before* you let our ride take off without us. Can we hide or are we making a run for it on foot?"

"Not here, Beth. They'll be on top of us any minute. And the last thing you want to do is shoot one of them."

"So you're just giving up?"

"We're surrounded with no way out. Tell 'em."

Beth got on the radio and gave their location and his decision. "We'll hold them off as long as we can."

He didn't have nearly enough ammo for a gunfight. Neither did Beth. As soon as she announced they were giving up, he turned off the satellite phone and shoved it in Beth's pocket.

"Are we going somewhere?"

"Down."

"But I thought—"

"I said that in case they were listening."

"Cluing me in on your plans might be nice." She stepped between the trees and around the large rock they'd grown around.

"No time. Can we talk about this later?"

"I'm supposed to be the big-time DEA agent and Mr. Rancher over here is..." Beth mumbled as she led the way.

Nick couldn't hear much of her complaints but got the gist. They were more about being caught unprepared than about him trying to save their behinds. That was just fine. She skidded along, grabbing rocks to slow herself, mad at their situation but not whining about it.

Maybe it was time to admit that he liked her more than just a little. But this was not the time or the place to admit it to her. A rock fell and hit his shoulder.

"Beth." He pointed up and behind them. "They're coming down."

"Then we need to move faster. Take the lead. I don't

suppose there's a cave or even a…a large crevice close by that we can use for cover?"

"Put your gun away. You need both hands for this. Stay close so I can get to you if you slip."

On a normal day, it would take several hours to just walk down the road to the bottom of this mesa. Coming straight down the side was dangerous. Very dangerous. They moved in silence. Breathing hard. No time for water. Their legs working overtime battling the steep descent.

Beth's legs were already sore from riding yesterday. She skidded, let out an "oh, no" and her hand landed in the middle of his back. He braced himself at her warning, catching a solid foothold and grip.

"These boots were not made for climbing." She brushed off the near fall with words, but she was stiff against the rock face.

"You might lose one or two of those rhinestones," he teased.

"We might fall to the bottom. Do you think I'd be better off climbing barefoot?"

"Better keep 'em on." He smiled and knew he needed to quit teasing. He should be serious. They were in deep trouble with no way out.

An avalanche of emotion dropped on his head like the rocks above them could at any moment. Thinking about the woman instead of the problem was a sure sign he liked Beth…a lot. Maybe too much.

Of course it was too much.

He anchored himself and held out his hand, ready for her to come to him. She hesitated, barely raising her arm. He latched on to her fingers and her feet moved slowly. He waited. Bodies close together, eyes level with his and wide with curiosity. A ray of sun broke through the clouds and turned them several shades lighter.

Men—bad men—were chasing them down a mountain. There was no place to hide. Nowhere to escape.

What did he do? He kissed her.

Not a good-bye. Not an invitation. Not just because she was close.

His girl was in his arms and her lips were smooth against his parched ones. Their tongues did a short dance and he felt more confident. She restored something in him that had been missing the past year. He lifted his head, unable to help the smile that spread across his face. He expected a stern set down from her about how they were in a hurry.

But, shoot, from the way she looked at him, maybe he'd given something back to her, too.

The wide-eyed moment was gone. She looked up and behind them, steadying herself with her hands on his shoulders. "We should probably get…"

"Moving. Right. You going to be okay?" he asked, really curious if the near fall had bothered her as much as the thought of losing her had bothered him.

Small rocks skittered past their heads. "Great. More than great. Excellent. Let's go while we can."

Choosing or creating a path where the javelinas didn't traverse was hard enough without the added thoughts about Beth. He could hear the grumbles about being caught off guard, about not doing her job, not protecting her asset.

"Is that me? Am I your asset?"

"Of course you are."

"Beth, I've told you this before. I can look after myself."

And just like it had been scripted, he heard the lone shot of a gun and zipped back to the cliff wall, covering Beth's body.

"There's something to be said about perfect timing." Beth drew her handgun from its holster.

"My father always says timing is the essence of all comedy, but there is nothing funny about getting shot. *Nada*." He took out his .38 from under his coat.

"We fired over your head, Burke," a man shouted from below them. Another bullet spat up dust next to Beth's feet. "Next time, maybe my man hits something that bleeds."

"Do you want to discuss this or will you admit that we're out of options?" Nick asked.

Beth whipped her head around, her hair wrapping itself around her neck. He stowed his gun at his back and lifted his hands into the air.

"Don't take too long," the stranger shouted. "You have an appointment with my boss."

"What if we just stay here?" Beth glanced at her watch. "I know it takes forever to get anywhere in this country, but shouldn't Pete and Cord be here soon? We've been climbing for an hour."

He shook his head. "It would take an hour to get to my place. Another forty minutes to get to the cabin, longer to get around to this side of the ridge. And that's if they brought ATVs like these guys."

"I don't believe this. There's got to be another way out of here."

He shook his head but didn't lose contact with her eyes. She had to know he was telling the truth. "We do what they say. We stay alive. We fight them later. Understand?"

"I didn't mean—" She shook her head. "We can't just give up."

"If you think I want to turn myself over to these guys, you're flat out wrong. I have a good idea what's going to happen to me. Just the thought of what they might do to you is already freezing my insides." He grabbed her shoulders, shaking her just a little before he stopped himself. "I know you can recover whatever they throw your way, but dying is worse. Dying is permanent."

Chapter Ten

Blindfolded, bound, knocked around and stuck on a chopper—Beth had thought the ride had been confined. Then they were dropped off in the middle of nowhere and stuck in a hole that wasn't as deep as one of her apartment closets.

"Do you think this cave is natural? It's barely big enough for an animal or one person. I can't believe they stuck us both in here." She shifted, attempting to relax her legs. There was barely room for them to sit hip to hip on a mixture of small stones and dirt. No more than five feet wide and four feet tall. Located in a remote gully it had a sturdy metal grate that locked in place across the front, seriously resembling a cage for a wild animal.

"Someone was probably searching for gold and started digging around this giant boulder. That's why it's such an odd shape. Rock above and below us, dirt all around."

Part of the rock was still jutting out of the so-called ceiling. Nick insisted on keeping it on his side. He also insisted on placing her at the back of the miniature cave. She would rather have been at the grate, watching their guards, searching for a way out.

"Or our friends out there just came onto park reserve land, discovered the beginnings of a hole in the side of a hill, put a grate in front of it and found themselves the perfect torture camp." His voice was low and gravely, sounding tired. "No one comes through this area, so they can pretty much do what they want. Ow, that smarts."

She was certain he was making fun of her question. Their captors had severely beaten him. More than once. The cut wasn't a laughing matter.

"I can't get the wound on the back of your head clean. If I use my fingers to pick the pebbles out… Well, my fingers are so dirty I'd probably be doing more harm than good." She squished herself backward. "Let me have the water to rinse it."

"No. We need to stay hydrated. It'll be okay," he said, tugging her hand away from the water bottle one of the men had tossed through the metal grate. "Get comfortable, honey. It's going to be a long night. My cut doesn't matter."

Nick didn't have to say why it didn't matter. He thought they were going to kill them—or at least him. At this moment, she couldn't argue that point. They were keeping them alive for someone and some reason. She wanted to be optimistic, but escaping from this hole didn't seem probable.

After one very long day, Beth was tired of breathing the smell of damp dirt on all sides of them. She'd never been an earthy kind of girl. Even the idea of her mother's patio garden escaped her.

A yoga mat and the strong smell of a chlorine pool would have been extremely hard to resist. She longed for a good stretch. Neither she nor Nick could sit with their backs straight because of the jagged ceiling. They couldn't extend their cramped extra-long legs. The only time they had relief from sitting on the hard rock was when the men dragged Nick outside the small hole to beat him.

Nick's wounds were getting worse. Each punch to his face broke open the previous scrapes. She hadn't known it was possible to bruise on top of a bruise. But the evidence was wrapped around her like a pretzel—the only way they both fit in the man-made cave.

Maneuvering wasn't easy, but they shifted to where they were sort of in each other's arms.

"This space is so tight it would be intolerable if we didn't like touching each other. At least they gave us back our coats." She arched her back, hitting her head on a protruding rock. "Ow."

"I'm glad you still have a sense of humor about all this." He pulled her in close against his light tan shirt that didn't hide any of the blood drips.

Some of his blood had stained her creamy yellow top. The very distinguishable smell of blood was easy to ignore mixed with their musk and dirt surroundings. She concentrated on Nick's body, searching for sore spots or wounds. She felt how relaxed and accepting he was. Or maybe they'd knocked his head one too many times and he was injured. He might not even know it.

"Are you nauseated at all?" She rubbed the back of her head. "I wonder if you have a concussion. Should you stay awake? Then again I think they changed that rule and you can sleep, but I have to make sure you wake up. But if you won't wake up, then what's the point of letting you fall asleep to wake you up later? That seems like it's defeating the purpose."

"I'm fine. Don't think too hard about it, just relax. I have a feeling it's going to be a rough night, and maybe we should rest while we can."

A gripping pain knotted her calf, making her jerk. She couldn't reach the cramp. All she could do was point her toes and that wasn't a huge success in her Western boots.

"Something wrong?"

She shook her head, gritting her teeth and determined

not to complain. "Do your muscles ache as much as mine? Wow, that was such a stupid question. How's the rib? Are you breathing okay?"

"Stop worrying about me. I protected the rib from another direct hit just like you taught me and reminded me during the last round. But I think you're right that it might be cracked."

When she'd yelled for him to cover his side, the big jerk hitting him had thrown extra punches to his arm. She'd keep her mouth shut next time. Now, too. She wouldn't complain. It was only a little muscle cramp.

"A cracked rib could be dangerous. The man in the dark brown coat drops his right shoulder when he's going to punch and always takes a step back for a running start when he's going to kick. The key is not to lose your balance and fall to the ground."

"Definitely, that's the key." He began to laugh, but winced. "Ow. Don't make me do that."

"I was only trying to help."

"Just knowing where you are is helping. I'll admit that I wish you were back at the ranch or even in Chicago, but since you aren't…" He squeezed her, bringing her in tight, then tipped her chin up so she met his eyes. "Do you really want me to stay awake?"

"No, you're right and I'm being overly cautious. Get some rest and sleep if you can."

"Not sure that's possible, but I'm leaning my head against this fool's gold and closing my eyes."

"We've been here all day and I hadn't noticed any pyrite."

"Now that it's dark," he tipped his head back to rest it on the stone, "the flashlights they shine in here are picking more of it up."

"Interesting."

"You don't sound very interested. Not the way you drew out the word like you were completely focused on something else. So what do you really want to talk about? Getting stuck here because of my decision to save our lives? What happened this morning during the storm? Or the scars?"

"Nightmares."

She was certain she heard several words she'd rarely repeat cursed softly across the top of her head. With her cheek resting lightly on his chest, she felt him swallow hard. His body was tenser than waiting for a kick in the ribs. She inched her knee closer to his back and ever so gently pushed him toward it.

"Relax. I know you don't think the nightmares are a big deal, but they are."

"Just because my mother put you up to this, doesn't mean you have to follow through. Does now seem like the right time? You going to use a two-hour DEA psychology course on me? Or maybe some half-forgotten college class? We'd be better off talking about the confusing geological formations here in Big Bend National Park."

"I'm sure the rock formations are spectacular, but how do you know this and why is it important at the moment?" He was very good at changing the subject, but so was she. She'd had years of practice with Elizabeth and Carroll, her parents. The always licensed and practicing psychotherapist professors.

"It's important." He lowered his voice. His lips brushed against her ear. "Because I worked a couple of summers here leading hikes. I know exactly where we're being held. So when we escape we won't be wandering in circles."

"Escape? Were you planning on telling me about these plans?"

Movement in their small space had to be confined and

coordinated. One person couldn't move without involving the other. So she felt every wince and hard intake of Nick's breath while he tried to come up with an answer, leaning his head back again. She noticed the split on his cheekbone bleeding. One of the men's obnoxious finger rings had cut him.

There was nothing she could do. He lifted his shoulder and smeared the blood. He didn't have an answer because he didn't have a plan. They were stuck until their situation changed. Hopefully for the better.

"Since escaping out of this hole isn't an option at this time—"

"It will be. The guards are lazy and the opportunity will be there. You'll just need to be ready to run."

"I thought fighting back wasn't a smart idea. Didn't you insist and make me agree before we were captured? We might be able to overpower these thugs in a fair fight. But there is nothing fair about someone pointing a .38 special at your head and forcing you to watch them beat up your boyfriend."

Oh, shoot. She'd called Nick her boyfriend. That couldn't be good. Had he heard her? Strangely enough, it didn't bother her at all to think of him that way.

"What?" he asked.

"Nothing. Um… Do you remember asking me what I wanted to talk about?" He didn't act like he heard her slipup, but changing the subject was good. "We're supposed to be talking about nightmares. I should probably answer your question of where I get my experience. It's quite legitimate."

"Spoken in the language of shrinks." He didn't bother disguising the distrust in his voice.

"I come by the speak honestly. I've spoken it fluently for years with my parents the therapists."

"I thought you were embellishing so I'd take your offer more seriously."

"I'm as serious as a heart attack, unfortunately. If Elizabeth didn't start analyzing why I was a foot model, Carroll would analyze why I practiced at the shooting range every day. But honestly, I wouldn't and couldn't talk to you like them. I can't pretend to have all the answers."

"Wait. I can't get over that you were a foot model. They really just used your feet? That's hilarious. I mean, I never would have imagined that you modeled." He laughed loud enough to draw the attention of their guards, who banged on the metal bars.

Nick kept silently laughing. She could feel his body shaking.

"I needed the money. Elizabeth and Carroll also teach at Northwestern and wanted me to attend there, but I wanted a criminal justice degree from Albany. That meant I had to pay for college."

"I went to Texas Tech."

"Modeling has its advantages. I almost always got to keep the shoes."

"That sure does explain the purple rhinestone boots." He chuckled and winced, holding his ribs.

"I like my boots."

"I'm sure you do. They just aren't…ideal for riding." He laughed again. "A foot model. Figures."

"What's that supposed to mean? Elizabeth and Carroll predicted this would happen." She'd said the wrong thing and he'd completely diverted the conversation to be about her. "I won't delicately coax you back to the real subject. It's my choice, so let's get back to the real topic. You. We were talking about your life and experiences. I know what it's like to lose sleep because I've had those nightmares."

"Not like mine."

"Granted, I wasn't shot in the back. But the trauma treatment is similar for losing a partner in a violent situation." She lowered her voice, not wanting to be overheard by their guards. "Why do you think the DEA sent me out here? I'm certain there are many more qualified agents suited for West Texas."

"Maybe."

"Is that reluctance in your voice to admit I'm right? Sweet, but it's unnecessary to stroke my ego. I like you anyway."

"Ha. Oh, man. I thought I asked you not to make me laugh. But you're right. There are a lot of things better than your ego that I'd rather stroke." He raised his right elbow in to her breast.

She was packed tight against the rear wall of their cell, but was able to shift and jam her left hand between their bodies, putting a stop to his intimate gesture. She had the perfect opportunity and couldn't allow herself to become distracted again.

"We're already in the mountains, so you can't run away this time to avoid a conversation. I really can help if you give me a chance."

"There's only one thing that will help me sleep better… finding the man who ordered my death. The prosecutor called me collateral damage, Beth. Said that the McCreas were the real target. I think he's wrong."

"I thought they caught and convicted the man responsible." She'd made a promise to Juliet and would get him to talk about the shooting. And if by some slim miracle they managed to escape, maybe he'd be on the road to seeking some professional help.

"Mac pulled the trigger, but I know someone else told him to. Someone besides Mac's boss."

"So you don't believe the reports or his testimony. For

the past year you've been trying to discover the person who ordered your shooting. Is that why you decided to teach me how to ride? So I'd help you on your hunt? Is that why you gave up so easily this morning? Do you think these men are responsible?"

"No."

Confident. Solid. Straight forward. No nonsense. All that strength in one little word, and she believed him. He'd never put anyone at risk on purpose.

"I have no illusions. I know it wasn't a favor for me. The threat from your mother about forcing you to leave the ranch, you believed her?" Actually, she'd believed the older woman's threat after only meeting her twice.

Which was one of the reasons she wanted Nick to talk about the shooting. Juliet deserved to have a few days when she didn't worry about him.

"I sure as hell did. When she sets her mind to something, it's gonna get done." Life popped back into his voice along with more of his Texas twang. "You better believe she would kick me out of the house. Everything I have is tied up in the cattle and ultimately the ranch. After Mac left—"

"You mean betrayed you. Mac Cauldwell betrayed you by working with the smugglers. Then he shot you in the back like a coward. He didn't *leave* you, Nick."

"I know that." He sounded hurt, not angry.

"Do you? The man was your mentor. He taught you to ride, rope, everything about a horse and especially how to run the ranch. You've suffered a horrible traumatic event. Why won't you consider speaking with a therapist or even the preacher at your church?"

Should she try to get him angry about the shooting instead of forgetting it? She wasn't a therapist like Carroll and Elizabeth, but she did have the questions her mother had supplied. She could guide him, help him sleep better. Maybe.

"My mom sure does like to share private matters."

"You realize that Mac made the choice to work with killers and then became one himself." It was difficult to keep her voice steady and not filled with anger for a dead man she didn't know. "In his testimony, he said it wasn't personal. He felt like he had nothing to—"

"It was personal to me," Nick said strongly in her ear.

"Of course it was."

He began shifting on their mutual rock. She wished she'd taken the coat off and sat on it. Her backside was growing numb. She hissed through her teeth as another cramp seized her calf.

"What's the matter?"

"Cramp," she eked out. He leaned forward and rubbed her leg as best as he could behind his back. "That position must be killing you. Here, sit up."

She liked Nick. He was a giving soul, a kind, considerate, thoughtful and brooding man. Yes, she liked him a lot. The physical attraction was self-explanatory after one look at him. He was tall and handsome, substantiating everything she'd heard about cowboys.

She had slept with him under a million stars and had made memories she wasn't likely to forget. But the other nights…

Like his parents, she'd heard the screams from his nightmares. The timing completely stunk, but he needed to face these demons. There wasn't any way she had enough knowledge to get rid of the anxiety that caused those horrible dreams. She could convince him he needed to visit someone who could.

"Look, I made a promise to your mom that I'd broach the subject." She didn't want to. Facing his demons made

her face a few of her own. In turn, that made her stomach hurt. "Can you answer some questions I got from my
mom? She mentioned that you'd have a better idea about
your anxiety. I mean about the dreams, about how to face
them. Then you could speak to your mother more knowl-
edgably."

The questions were part of a common test used to determine if someone might be suffering from post-traumatic
stress disorder. Should she mention that both of her parents had insisted she give up the idea of talking with Nick?

Both had been surprised to hear from her last week.
She rarely called. Her fault, not theirs. They respected her
space. Most of the time she was too embarrassed to chat.
Her failure was always on her mind when she faced them.

If she didn't get her act together and get them out of this
hole, she'd completely wash out of the DEA.

Or she'd be completely dead.

Chapter Eleven

"What do you want to know about the nightmares?" Nick asked when everything was silent.

Beth's nightmares of the shooting in Chicago drove her to practice every day. There had been incidents in her career involving gunfire. That day had been different. The reports of other team members had blamed her for her partner's death. All she could remember was the hesitation. She didn't know why it had happened. But she'd never hesitate again. Never miss. Never be punished and sent to the wilds of West Texas again.

"I want to ask you questions, and I want you to answer honestly and then give your answers some thought. It might help. I'm not making any guarantees."

Her parents had insisted on therapy on top of speaking to the doctor assigned by the department. She probably would have ignored both if one hadn't been mandated for her to get back to work. She was more familiar with family concerns than she wanted to admit to Nick.

"Might as well." He shrugged. "I don't think you're going to sleep, which means you're going to keep me awake."

"Okay, so we already know you suffered a violent event and you have nightmares." She needed to recall the important questions that would make him realize the truth.

"You've also distanced yourself from people and do nothing but work from dawn to dusk."

"What does that have to do with anything? Of course, I work. Anyone I hire to take Mac's place could be working for these creeps. So I take care of things myself."

"So, I guess the answer to if you have trouble trusting people is yes."

"I trust you." He leaned forward far enough to nip her neck and then lick the saltiness off his lips.

The gesture seemed very innocent until she could see the teasing in his eyes. Or was that deliberate temptation?

"I'm not going to be distracted. So let's get back to my questions. Do you feel normal?" The rest of that particular question was: do you feel like you want a family and children. Asking that at this point in their relationship might give him the wrong impression.

"What I feel is cramped, sore and beat up. Wouldn't you say our situation is a little different than my everyday normal?"

"You know what I'm asking. Before today, during the past year. Could you go about ranch business thinking long term?"

"I, um…" He tilted his face toward the bars of their cage, and his muscles tensed beneath her fingers.

"Be honest, Nick. There's no one else here and I'm not going to tattle back to your mother. Besides, I shared my modeling secret with you."

He released a deep sigh. "All right. Long term? No. Not without knowing why it happened."

"The next question. Do you try to avoid thinking about the shooting? And do you relive it when you pass where it happened?" She'd seen him take the long way around the paddock to the barn and had even caught his long stare at the corral.

"I almost get through a day and then look at the corral… I freeze, go right back to the shooting and almost pass out. Only way for me to cope is to take off to the mountains."

His voice was intense but quiet. Rough but emotional. She didn't want to force him to relive it, but there was no other way to move past it.

"Of course, I try not to think about it, but the more I try *not* to think about, the more I do. You already know that we're here, right here, because I wanted away from where it happened."

"These men came looking for us, Nick. It's not your fault."

Nick watched the last rays of sunshine fade behind the canyon walls. It was the weird time of twilight before everything got so dark that you couldn't see. The guards weren't as diligent as before about watching the hole. But there was no way to dig out or lift the iron grate unless it was unlocked.

At least they weren't hurting Beth. He could see the strategies brewing behind her beautiful eyes each time they were dragged from the cave. She'd remind him how to protect himself and he'd remind her not to try to escape.

"I have to tell you something," he whispered, turning to look at her in the fading light. "I, um…I took that test you're asking me. Several times. Enough to pretty much have it memorized."

Beth's dark eyes were huge and questioning him. "You're just saying that so I'll stop."

"Have I had outbursts of anger? Have I had difficulty concentrating? Do I feel guilty? Feel jumpy? Feel hyper vigilant, constantly ready for any threat? I think I should answer no on that one, seeing how we're in this mess. You and mom dropped enough hints."

"Why didn't you say anything?"

He shrugged. "Don't know. So what if I answered yes to most of the questions? So what if I'm having a little trouble sleeping? What's a shrink going to tell me that I don't already know?" He tightened his arms, to hold her next to him and keep her from untangling their semi-comfortable position.

If the notion of pulling away from him wasn't ridiculous, he could have sworn that's what her squirming was trying to accomplish. But the space was too small for them to move more than a couple of inches either way.

"I can't believe you played me like that. And therapists really can help you understand what's happening and how to deal with it."

"Whoa, whoa, whoa." He leaned back until he could see the fire make her eyes sparkle. Or was that just the fight in her dark blue eyes? "I wasn't *playing* you. And I've got a pretty clear idea of what's happening. There aren't a lot of options at the moment."

"If you weren't playing along, why didn't you tell me when I first broached this subject that you'd already self-diagnosed and are going to ignore it?"

"Because I didn't mind you asking. I wasn't excited about it, but I didn't mind." Her body relaxed against his again. "Mom needs to stop worrying about me. *You* should stop worrying. I'm old enough to take care of myself."

He should start worrying about how they were going to get out of there. They needed a plan.

"By the way, it wasn't your mom who filled me in. Kate did," she said.

"Kate? I should have guessed." His voice had that slight quality of grief to it that he hated.

"Do you still love her?"

"Huh? My mom?"

"Don't play dumb with me. I know there's an intelligent man hiding behind that laid-back cowboy exterior."

Nick searched her eyes in the dimming light. Then he kissed her. Busted lip, sore jaw, twisted into a position he didn't think possible, he kissed her some more. Deep, strong and long, she kissed him back. He raised his outside arm to her cheek, dusted at a smudge of dirt, hooked a long wavy curl behind her ear and felt desire burn in his gut.

No, he'd never really loved Kate. Could he tell Beth that? Should he tell her that he hadn't realized it until she'd asked?

Neither the dirt around them nor the men standing outside threatening their lives mattered. He explored her lips, aware of her soft breasts pressed against his sore body. He and Beth were packed in like cattle being hauled to auction. He didn't care. Something clicked... And then he fell.

Hard.

After all these years thinking there was one perfect woman for him and that she loved someone else. This moment was a wakeup call. He'd fallen for someone who was all wrong for a cattleman. From the moment he'd met Beth at Pete's ranch and she'd looked petrified at the size of the calmest animal he owned, he'd been attracted.

Frustrated and attracted like he'd never allowed himself to be before. But, come on, she still couldn't ride a horse and didn't really want to. They took a breath, resting their foreheads together.

"I would have said you were smart last week if I'd known you could kiss like that."

"I've kissed you before." He couldn't stop searching her face for a... He didn't know what. He just couldn't stop looking at her.

"Not like that," she answered so breathlessly that he had to kiss her again.

The butt of a gun hitting the bars to their cage broke them slightly apart. The guard slung the strap back over his shoulder and walked away, laughing.

"You should try to get some shut-eye."

"And what about you?" she asked, yawning.

"I'll be okay, Beth. Don't worry so much."

How did she manage to rub his back in their confinement? He didn't need to know, he just enjoyed it.

Beth's hand stopped moving a couple of minutes later. He wanted to shift and make her more comfortable, but it wasn't possible. Her body relaxed, her breathing deepened and she was finally asleep. Maybe the guards would wait a couple of hours before beating him again so she could get some rest.

With all the talk about his nightmares he couldn't close his eyes. No one was watching them. The guards sat around a fire that burned inside a fifty-gallon drum. Sparks flew up toward the black sky. No moonlight. No stars.

Shoot, there was still some sleet on the ground that had been in the shade all day. And it was just going to get colder out in the open like they were. The wind whipped through the gully, straight into their little hole. It would probably snow again before morning.

He inched his hand to an iron bar. He lifted, but it barely budged. He thought he'd seen a lock at the top. They were isolated. No one would venture to this gully. Just like no one normally rode through the part of his land they used to smuggle drugs.

Why here? Camouflaged tarps protected their captors from an aerial spotting. Weather and remoteness protected them from accidental trespassers. They hadn't asked Beth or him anything. Why keep them alive? He wasn't DEA or the law, but he was smart enough to know someone probably wanted information.

That was the million-dollar question. And what would happen when the men got their answer? They'd be dead this time tomorrow. All because he couldn't stand to look at the place where he'd already died.

Chapter Twelve

They'd been held captive in the hole for a day and a half. They were unbound while inside their earth cage, but their muscles were one endless spasm. The helplessness seeped into each of Beth's thoughts like the damp cold had through her jeans.

The men continued to beat Nick, kicking him before they could straighten their legs and stand. Afterward, Nick would pull her into his arms, warming and comforting her. Wincing a great deal, but still comforting her.

Their relationship had changed and would never be the same. They had a strong attraction and they'd slept together twice. Yet it was his soothing protectiveness that she'd never needed or desired before that she wanted more of. Which was totally ridiculous, because that might mean she wanted more of what was happening to them and that was far from the truth.

Seeing them attack Nick over and over was hell. None of the men laid a hand on her other than a shove to get her moving or holding her back while they laughed and hit Nick. She'd wished several times that she didn't have to witness the horrifying things they were doing to someone she cared about. But she'd admitted to herself that it would be much worse captured and alone.

It was late afternoon when two Jeeps bounced over the

trail toward the makeshift camp. Their captors shoved her toward one while dragging Nick into the other. Once out of the gully, they drove east for twenty minutes from the cave—she'd noted the time on the car clock. Not only in case Nick, her new partner, needed some help determining their position, but also so she could find it again.

Nick appeared to be semiconscious, his head sagging to his chest as two men dragged him from the other vehicle. Fresh blood trailed from the cut above his brow. The skin close to his eyes had turned a sickly dark purple. She couldn't be certain—because they wouldn't let her touch him—but it looked as if his nose had been broken during the last round of punching.

Several armed men were posted around a large Spanish-style home in the middle of nowhere. There were no telephone lines or power cables. Yards and yards of trees had been removed. No one could breach the perimeter without being seen. Even the brush had been cleared away, making it impossible to approach or leave without being detected.

Escape was looking harder and harder.

They were escorted around the side of the house. She had two huge beasts on either side of her. Nick's toes left deep drag marks on the gravel path as he was being pulled behind her. There were beautiful flowers, lush landscaping, tennis courts at the far end of the compound and a swimming pool.

The hot tub looked especially inviting to her sore muscles. Fog billowed from the cold air hitting the hot water. She could imagine soaking and warming up her frozen bones.

A man rose from the bubbles and was met with his robe and slippers as he stepped onto the patio. He knotted the belt around his waist and took a brandy glass from a tray that miraculously appeared at his elbow. He looked very debonair, very comfortable and very definitely in charge.

"Why are you doing this to us? What do you want?"

Beth's heart beat like a crazy woman's on crack. This was the first time they'd seen the man giving orders, the one their captors referred to as Bishop.

"I would say welcome to my home, *senorita*, but I am not acting as a host tonight. You and Nick Burke have been an unnecessary distraction requiring too much of my time."

Multiple guards walked by with growling dogs. A constant reminder that it would be impossible to outrun them. As weak and tired as they were, the dogs would surely catch them. They'd never climb the stone walls that were at least eight feet tall, a foot thick topped with barbed wire.

When she made it back to the task force, she'd be able to pick this location out from satellite photos. But first they had to make it to Marfa and Nick's home. And that wouldn't be easy since she was certain they'd crossed the border into Mexico.

"Okay, I get the intimidation tactics. What do you want?" She was free, could make a break and disarm one of the guards, but not both. Then what would they do? Nick looked as if he could barely move. Would running back to the Jeeps be a brilliant idea or a suicide mission?

Bishop hovered closer, having to look slightly up at her as he stalked her like a dead-eyed shark. No, a buzzard. He wouldn't make the kill. He would just circle until he could swoop in for the sick feast.

"Bring them to the pool," Bishop commanded and flicked his hand.

A blonde woman stood at the two open French doors to the house. Lacy curtains blew around her legs. Backlit as she was, she looked otherworldly. Was the blonde important? Wife? Girlfriend? Partner? She stepped through the doors, pulling them shut behind her.

It was hard to believe this place belonged to a gangster or member of the Mexican cartel. Beth didn't know what organization Bishop was a part of. She needed to do her job and find out, because when they escaped—and they would escape—she would bring every law enforcement agency possible down on this guy's head to take him out.

She stretched her fingers wide at her side, realizing they were numb from clenching them into fists for so long. She relaxed her shoulders, stretched her neck. She'd be aware and prepared to act at any moment.

The perimeter into the unknown was out. Not a single gate except where they'd driven through. Nothing but lawn furniture and pool toys. After two days of little sleep and less food, she wouldn't be able to break any of it fast enough to improvise a weapon.

Bishop crossed to the deep end of the pool. With a flick of his wrist he indicated where she should stand and gave a nod to his men.

"Let's cut to the chase. Why don't you just tell us who you work for or even what you want. Then we won't have to wonder about it anymore."

Bishop looked amused but quickly returned to his stoic expression. He didn't bother to answer either.

It was another cold, cloudy late afternoon, but nothing compared to Chicago. The weather shouldn't have fazed her. She shivered for Nick when they jerked his heavy coat down, pinning his hands behind his back. His shirt was ripped open and sliced from his body. Her shiver wasn't from the weather. She was afraid of what might finally happen. If only Nick were okay they could fight back.

As their breaths formed small patches of fog as it left their mouths, Nick lifted his head slightly and winked. She was dizzy with relief that he was at least coherent. She faced Bishop, who had pulled a chair closer to the pool's edge. "Please tell me what you want. Is it money? Are we being ransomed?"

Portraying the damsel in distress was easy at this point. Nick needed medical attention and the fear in her voice was real on every level as she wondered how they'd get out of this predicament.

"I don't think the United States government will pay for either of you. They always say they won't negotiate. I do not believe your chances would be very good."

"What? I...I don't understand. Don't you want money from Nick's family?"

"No. I need something else from Burke. Something he neglected to do last year." Bishop smiled slowly, dipping his head to his chin.

"What are you talking about?"

"Die. He needs me to die," Nick groaned. "With me dead, he can force out my parents and take my land."

"It won't be that easy," she said, not believing for one minute that Nick's parents would just give up.

"I'm sorry, *querida*. Do you hope to convince me of something? I find it so very easy to set my eyes on a goal and obtain."

"Why haven't you just shot us then?"

"We need to know about this task force you are a part of. How much has the Rook told to you?"

She shook her head. "I don't know what you're talk-ing—"

Bishop slapped her check, snapping her head to the left. He'd taken her by surprise. She'd been totally unprepared for an attack. The sting made her skin burn and her eyes water. She would have fought harder to stop the tears if she'd shown her badge as a DEA agent. But at the moment, playing her part as Nick Burke's fiancée, her tears fell.

"Do not waste my time, Agent Conrad. I know the two of you are involved with the *policia* and not each other. But if you would like to play the game, by all means, let's play. You remember *The Newlywed Game, si*? You say you are his *prometido*, then answer *rapido*. What did Burke's father do before buying their ranch?"

He waved his hand and the guard standing next to Nick shoved him into the pool.

Beth was midair, almost in the water, when a thick arm yanked her backward. She spun around. "What are you doing? He can't surface! He'll drown with his hands pinned behind his back." As exhausted as Nick already was he wouldn't be able to tread water for long.

"Yes. Answer."

Around the struggle, the water turned a pale pink, washing the blood from Nick's skin. The guard that had knocked Nick into the deep end knelt at the edge and prevented Nick from kicking off the bottom to surface. Whenever he struggled and kicked to get air, the man shoved him down again.

"Alan was… Oh God, we… Nick and I haven't spoken about his parents, especially what they did before moving here." The answer was in his file. *Think. Think. Think.* Whatever he'd done, he'd retired early. "Please let him up."

"I should warn you, one wrong answer and he does not resurface."

"I think Alan sold his company. They made machines that made other tool machines. Something like that."

Bishop nodded. The man grabbed a handful of Nick's hair and yanked upward. Nick gasped, sucking in air. He tossed his head from side to side attempting to get released.

"What did your father do before ranching?" Bishop asked as politely as making casual conversation at tea.

Nick sank, pushed off the bottom and broke the surface again, sputtering at the surface. "Machine—" he coughed and spat water "—tooling company."

Bishop's man grabbed Nick's dark teak hair, bobbing him up and down like laundry on a washboard. Nick kicked and struggled to get his mouth above the freezing water. Each time he got close to getting a deep breath, Bishop's man sent him under.

"Let him up. We both answered."

"Next question. What is Nick's favorite food?"

Nick was released and sank. The longer she took to consider an answer, the longer he went without oxygen.

"Biscuits," she said with little confidence, taking a wild guess. The second guard pulled her around her waist again, yanking her back against his chest. Without realizing it, she'd been inching closer to the pool's edge. "Let him up."

Bishop nodded once again. Nick answered correctly and the questions continued, the near-drowning repeated and repeated. He struggled less, succumbing to Bishop's man holding him by his hair as the sun fell behind the surrounding mountains.

"Last question, Agent Conrad. What has the task force discovered from Mr. Rook?"

Nick was shoved under the water again. Then Bishop jerked her head toward him, his fingers biting into her cheeks.

"We can't answer something we don't know." She wanted to scream, fight, lie. Anything to get Nick out of the water.

"Are you still denying you were brought here by the DEA?"

"I'm here because I love Nick. Why would the DEA

send anyone here that can't even ride a horse?" She raised her hands, covering Bishop's who still tugged at her chin forcing her to look at him instead of the pool. "Please, I'm begging you, let him up."

With one glance at his guard, Bishop's man allowed Nick to float away from the edge. Face down.

"What have you done?" She broke free and ran to the pool.

The guard reached for Nick, but missed. He swiped at the water again, but the cattleman's body sank to the bottom. Then, he shoved off the bottom shooting out of the water, bare chested and hands free. With one hard tug the guard who had been holding her let go and toppled into the pool. Nick disappeared under the water again, wrestling the big man like an overstuffed crocodile.

Between the light, waves and bubbles it was difficult to distinguish who was winning. Bishop's hand was suddenly around her neck. She tried to pry his fingers loose, but he had a firm, strong grip and jerked her to her feet.

Nick pulled his opponent to the steps at the opposite end of the pool. The guard who had been holding him under joined them on the steps. Nick dodged a punch and stepped from the water, dripping but steady, the guards splashing behind him. He brushed his hand across his face, never breaking eye contact with her.

"We aren't part of any task force," he said to Bishop, resting his hands on his knees. "I supplied horses for the sheriff, and Beth was stubborn enough to insist on going with me. She wanted to show off for my old girlfriend."

The pressure around her throat increased. The instinct to claw at Bishop's hands to release herself overtook her. She couldn't budge his grasp. The soft bones in her neck cracked as if they were about to break. She wanted to get free, grab a gun and shoot the son of a b—

Nick's whiskey-colored eyes reassured her to stay calm. Why the heck did she believe it would be okay just by looking at him? But she was sure it would, so she relaxed, taking short shallow breaths.

"Are we through playing this sick version of an out-of-date game?" Nick asked before a third guard appeared and placed a gun against his head.

Bishop relaxed his grip, but kept her as a barrier between him and everyone else. "Perhaps your girlfriend needs a little more enticement to talk. Shoot him in the leg, but not too severe. I don't want him to bleed out. Yet."

The guard he'd wrestled in the pool grabbed a gun and aimed at Nick's hip.

"Wait! I am DEA, but I haven't had access to Rook. None. Don't have your answers." Shoved forward, she stumbled but stayed on her feet close to Nick and the two guns. "Are you going to torture me now?"

If Bishop said yes and she took Nick's place would she be able to handle it? Would her training be enough to keep her tongue from wagging?

"What gave you the impression I was not already?"

Her punishment had been watching them slowly drown Nick. Would they kill him now that she'd admitted her status? Then what? After they had the information they wanted, would she be killed, too?

"You can do whatever you want to the both of us. It still won't change the fact that we have no information on anyone referenced as Rook. That wasn't my objective. Finding scum like you was," she answered without sharing her exact mission.

She watched the surprise flash into his cold eyes. He stifled it quickly.

"Take them back to the holding cell." He looked toward

the French doors where a woman's silhouette appeared. "I need to consult about this decision."

While Bishop motioned for the guards to move forward, Nick pressed something sharp into her hand and she slid it into her coat pocket. A blade. Nick had fought with the guard under water to get his knife.

He'd just stolen their ticket home.

Chapter Thirteen

The pain in his lungs was excruciating, but Nick had kept it together on the return walk to the front of the house. The men at his sides had kept a death grip on his biceps. Now they talked around him, admiring the fight, complaining about another night in the cold tent, wanting to finish their job and be reassigned somewhere there were women.

Beth caught his eye, raised her eyebrows and tapped her pocket where the knife was hidden. He shook his head, crossing his fingers that she'd wait until they were back at the gully. When she stretched her neck just like she always did before firing her weapon, every muscle in his body tensed, ready. But she continued walking between her escorts.

They were separated into the two Jeeps they'd arrived in. Waiting to attack was better. They'd be that much closer to the border when they escaped. That much closer to finding help. He watched her get into the backseat without a word or glance in his direction.

Beth would know they should make their move before they were back in their cage. But did she have it inside her to use the knife and not second-guess herself?

His hands were secured in front of him with a thin nylon rope that cut into his flesh. He understood most of the conversation spoken in Spanish. While the two guards talked, he painfully pulled and stretched the nylon cord to a workable length.

Fortunately, the two men he'd sent for a swim had stayed behind. The guys were betting on who would win in a no-rules fight—Nick or the overgrown wrestler he'd taken to the bottom of the pool.

The wrestler, named Ricky, would win according to the driver because he'd kill Nick the next time he saw him. The other guard agreed, because Nick had let both of the men live earlier.

Yeah, the nice guy in him had come out in spite of his anger over nearly being killed or about confronting the man who wanted him dead. He'd thought about it for a split second, but hadn't been able to leave the guard to drown. The next time he wouldn't think twice. He'd think about being shot at the corral and slowly bleeding out, his thoughts and vision fading to nothing. He'd remember how they would kill Beth if they didn't get out of this mess.

The jerks in the front thought it would be fun to ride with the windows down to freeze his wet body. He took deep lungsful of air, coughing up water in the process. He shook himself, getting the blood circulating throughout his body—especially his hands—and becoming more alert.

As they bounced over the rutted tracks that led back to their camp, he tugged off each boot and dumped the water that had pooled inside. He'd be able to run now, instead of slosh his way to freedom.

Completely cognizant of his whereabouts during this trip, he confirmed where they were on the map in his head. On foot from the camp and in the dark, it would take him about three hours to make it back to the US to find help. Then again, he wasn't alone, it *was* dark and he was injured. Without a compass in this cloud cover, it would be harder to travel off the hiking trails. Finding help would be more difficult since it wasn't exactly the most popular season for camping.

One thing at a time.

"Hey," he called. Then in the most broken Spanish he could manage, because he didn't want them to know he was nearly fluent, *"Habla. Usted. Inglés?"*

Escape first. Then solve each problem.

"Sure, man. We're from Port Aransas," the driver said, receiving a punch in the arm from his passenger. "What? He can't tell anyone if he's dead tomorrow."

"Well, before you kill me I need to take a leak."

"It's your turn to take him. I'm going to grab a smoke when we get back. It don't make sense that Bishop don't allow smoking," the driver complained to his partner.

"Whatever, man. I need a smoke, too."

The camp was within sight. The four guards with them had been the most complacent of the group. Nick was betting they wouldn't be expecting an attack. Or at least he hoped they wouldn't. His two guards might have laughed when the water from his boots had hit the floorboard or when he'd allowed the other guards to live. They wouldn't be snickering when he used his tied wrists as a weapon.

Short breaths got his blood pumping even more. He focused his mind on a picture of Beth... Blood spreading across her beautiful chest. *Focus.* He had to do this. They'd already admitted that he and Beth would be dead tomorrow.

The Jeep stopped. The passenger guard jumped out, gun still at the back waist of his pants. He lit his cigarette as he went.

Now! He had to make his move now.

He soared forward, arms high. The rope cut across the windpipe of the driver before the man knew what had hit him. Nick watched the guard's eyes in the mirror, felt the man's fingernails digging into his flesh as he tried to pull Nick's hands away. The driver lost consciousness before the second guard realized they weren't getting out.

Beth's Jeep parked behind theirs. The lights cut off just as his backseat door flew open. "Come on. Do you need to take a leak or what?"

Cigarette smoke wafted into the vehicle. Nick waited for him to lean through the door, rolling as close to the backseat as he could get. The guard held his gun with his right hand and reached inside with his left. Nick kicked the free arm up and back into the roof. He heard the bone snap and the man screamed in pain. There were shots—both from his gun and from behind him.

He focused on the image of Beth hurt and bleeding. The conjured picture was all he allowed himself to see. They had to escape before his imagination became her reality. Kicking out again, he connected with the man's chest, knocking him backward.

Nick ignored the man's painful cries. He ignored his own cracked ribs as he slid across the seat and stepped onto the guards back, keeping his face in the dirt. The guard continued to scream and fire his weapon, but he was unable to twist his arm toward his attacker.

Soon the gun was empty and Nick heard dry clicks. Before he could kick the man unconscious, he smelled gas.

Where was the cigarette?

The same instant, the leaking fuel ignited and Nick could only run. He searched the darkness for Beth. The fire was soon bright enough to see her long hair blowing in the wind on the far side of the second vehicle.

More screams drew his attention behind him. The guard he'd had in the dirt was running toward the camp. Beth's driver slumped toward his window, unmoving. "Beth!" She was struggling with her second guard outside her Jeep.

As Nick drew closer he saw the knife in Beth's hand. The man was holding it away from slicing his body. And she was holding his gun away from pointing at her. Nick used one of the moves she'd taught him and put pressure on the guard's hand to drop the gun.

It fell to the ground with a whelp of agony as the guard's arm bent backward, giving Beth the advantage she needed. With her free hand she turned the knife. The man lunged and then stopped just as quickly. He fell to the ground, eyes wide in death, the knife stuck in his chest.

"Are you all right, Nick?" Beth asked, out of breath as she knelt and wiped the blade clean on the guard's jacket.

"Yeah. What about my driver?"

The flames and smoke were curling in through the window. The driver hadn't moved since he'd choked him.

"He's not dead?" She took a step around him, ready to rescue their enemy.

"It's okay." They locked eyes. He didn't know what he felt. Remorse. Guilt. Relief maybe. A man was dead by his hands, and he mainly felt confused.

"We need to get out of here before that fire hits the gas tank. Get in… I'll drive." She ran to the other side of the old Jeep, stopping at the back wheel. "How far can we get on a flat tire? Can we change it?"

"I don't think we have time. One of my guys got away." He picked up the pistol and pulled the light windbreaker from the dead man. He held onto his ribs as they both ran away from the camp. "We need to keep quiet, run hard and get as far away as possible."

"Trade you." She held out the knife to him as they slowed to climb from the gully. "I'm better with a gun."

"You looked pretty damned good with that knife, too." He gave her the gun. She released the magazine to reveal two bullets. "I'm not exactly wearing anything to carry weapons. Why don't you keep it in your coat pocket?"

"Okay."

The explosion rocked them as they reached the top of the ridge. It lit up the surrounding sky.

"If the guard who escaped hasn't contacted anyone yet, Bishop is sure to know something's up now. He'll be sending people here on the double to check out that explosion."

"Then we better pick up our pace if we want to stay ahead of them to the border," she said as he boosted her up a steep incline.

He hid the wince, letting her go in front of him a minute so he could get control of the hitch in his side. He'd have to bury the pain, push through it, and not care that the evidence on his chest reminded him he'd lost this battle before.

No, this time he had Beth to worry about. Passing out wasn't an option. If he did, she'd never make it out of the desert alive.

Chapter Fourteen

Bishop should have ordered their deaths. Of course he could at any time. One call and it would be done. He'd never know how or where the bodies would reside for eternity. Nick Burke and Beth Conrad wouldn't be a problem any longer.

But he couldn't do that.

They were a problem.

His partners wanted answers. All he'd achieved this evening was raising more questions. He sat at the hot tub's edge, warming his feet occasionally, but it was time to go inside.

"You're still up?" He wrapped his arms around the slim waist of Patrice Orlando. "You should have joined me outside."

"You looked deep in thought. Did you get the answers you needed?" She picked up the toppled king from a chessboard. "I've never understood the fascination you men have with this game."

Bishop lifted the long blond hair off her neck, letting the straight locks flow over his fingers. "Sex with you is always a pleasure. A welcome interruption to the isolation of this horror factory where I currently reside. I enjoy our time together. Don't you?"

"I'm here for your pleasure. You know that. You also

should remember that this *horror factory* as you call it is much better than the slum where you grew up."

He kissed her sweet-scented neck, wanting to forget the poverty-stricken image. He never forgot. It was one of the reasons he continued to stay isolated, without any real connections.

"I use that memory to my advantage every day, Patrice. I surround myself with men who have families in the same circumstances from which I came. I know what they are willing to do for their families. They are loyal to me. Perhaps that is something *you* should remember."

He took the black king from her hand and replaced it on the onyx board. He kept their bodies close as he rearranged the pieces, segregating the red from black. Once done, he spanned Patrice's slim hips and flat stomach. She was a superb work of physical art. Very deserving of the time he'd take exciting every inch of her.

"I think you treat your men like the pawns on this silly chess board. You expect their loyalty. They guard the king, the rook and the bishop like they're loyal subjects." She took a pawn and rolled it between her palms. "All the while, you forget that if moved as far as they can go, they exchange themselves for the most powerful piece on the sidelines. That's rarely a rook or bishop, right?"

There was something unpleasant about the way she said his name as if he was any other playing piece. "I thought you didn't play chess."

"Oh, no. I said I have never understood the fascination with the game that some people have." She took a step to his second board where he awaited his opponent's next move. "Have you considered sacrificing your queen here?"

It would be a bold move. He rapidly scanned the pieces, mentally mapping the moves and countermoves. He could possibly achieve check in four moves. There was much more to Patrice Orlando than a good sex partner.

"Enough small talk." He spun her around and latched his lips on hers, rocking his hardness into her. Ready to take advantage of all the time she'd remain there before returning to his partners in Texas.

The pawn she'd been holding dropped and rolled across the floor.

She kissed him solidly, forcibly, confidently. Her long nails left their sting on his chest while tugging open his robe. He yanked up her skirt, ready to throw her over the edge of the couch and take her.

An explosion split the isolated silence of his world.

"What was that?" Patrice asked.

"It is the DEA agent and her cattleman." He lashed the robe's belt into place, yelling for the men stationed outside the French doors. Somehow the couple had escaped. He wasn't lucky enough to believe they had been killed, ending the debate of his partners.

"What are we going to do? You know his land is essential for next week's shipping endeavors." She straightened her skirt, not at all disconcerted that three gawking men intently watched her actions.

"They should have allowed me to kill them both when they were here. Now we waste valuable time hunting them down again. Ridiculous," he scoffed.

"But it's what our associates wanted. We must discover if the Rook has betrayed us."

"Who is the best tracker we have?" he asked the two men who had been bested by Burke earlier. Both should have been punished for letting the weaker man take them by surprise. He had not thought what would be best. A horseback ride in the dark would be sufficient for now.

"I'm not certain, Mr. Bishop. We don't do a lot of chasing around here," one of the guards replied.

Bishop crossed the room and backhanded the man. "I did not ask what we don't do. You've had it too easy. I'll make certain your family knows how lax you have been. Is that what you want from me?"

"No, sir, Mr. Bishop. I'll find someone for you."

"You mean for you." He pointed at the man and the one who stood beside him. "You're both going with him. Now get out."

The two men Burke had fought with left the room, leaving his best man shaking his head in the corner.

"Do you disagree, Michael?"

"No. But before you ask me to kill those two, *senor*, all the men have grown soft. It's been a while since they've had to work for something. This will be good for them, I think."

"It's bothersome. You'll have to pursue on horseback. Transport them to the holding camp and clean up the mess that is there. I'm certain it is a big mess after that explosion. Stay in touch via the satellite phones. Bring me back the *Americanos*. Alive or dead." He shrugged. "But dead is preferable."

Michael left to set things in motion. Patrice had fetched the runaway pawn and replaced it. She tapped her nail against her cheek, seemingly deep in thought.

"Let's head to bed, Patrice. They won't find them in the dark unless my incompetent men managed to shoot them at the camp."

Patrice circled the room, turning the locks on the doors as she passed. "I can't stay much longer now, hon. This change of events needs to be reported as soon as I can drive back. But it is the middle of the night."

She unzipped her skirt and let it fall to the floor. Afterward she lifted one high heel out of the soft pile and then the other. She tugged the small, stretchy shirt over her head. Her long blonde hair fell down her back as she dropped the material on the carpet. She pulled the curtains on the doors, but not before showing off her perfect store-bought boobs to the passing guard.

"They'll be impatient for the results of your search, so it might be better to delay delivering the message."

Then she was his for the night. He unbelted his robe, slipped from his swim trunks and knew it would be a sleepless yet exciting night.

Chapter Fifteen

Nick turned down a path, heading due east from what she could tell. Beth didn't question his direction or complain about the pace. He was the one injured and with only a windbreaker in just above freezing temperatures. They jogged until the terrain and darkness made it impossible to move quickly. Yet it was still hard on them both. He knew where he was going. At least he looked like he knew.

She, on the other hand, was completely turned around after a few minutes with no moonlight to mark their direction. She'd be totally lost without him. They had to push themselves, but he had to remember his injuries.

"Don't you need to slow down or rest?"

"Are you tired?" His voice was full of concern for her, yet he held his left arm next to his ribs. "Want to stop a couple of minutes?"

If she said she was exhausted, it would sound like she was concerned for herself, not the other way around like she'd intended. As long as she thought he wasn't pushing too hard, she'd keep up with him.

"I was actually thinking about you and your injuries. I mean, to be quite frank, you practically drowned a couple of hours ago."

"A lot of that was show. I was working my arms free."

It certainly hadn't looked like much acting had been

involved. That was as close to a real drowning as she ever wanted to be. He had to be lying, but she couldn't wound his pride by calling him out. "Oh, well, that's such a relief."

The quick sharp look on his face and narrowing of his eyes was apparent even in the low, almost nonexistent light. So were the bruises on his tanned skin and his swollen, most likely broken, nose.

"Hey, there wouldn't happen to be any convenience stores around the next corner. Would there?" With two therapists for parents, levity wasn't her strong suit, but she could try. "I'd even settle for a small stream so I can wet my throat."

They were resting on yet another rock. This place was full of them. She was in the process of leaning back to stretch aching muscles when Nick's arm darted out to stop her.

"Watch it. There's prickly pear."

"As in cactus? That would have been a disaster. Thanks."

His face was close and puzzled. Her heart beat faster anticipating his next move. More so than when they'd been at Bishop's fortress. She was more aware of her reaction to him now, wanting him to be close all the time. After sharing the confining space of their cave, it was a little weird to be able to move in any direction she wanted without consulting him.

"I...um...I need part of your shirt. I'd use mine but..." Shrugging and pointing to his bare chest, he leaned down, took the edge and used his teeth to start a rip. The air warmed and floated across her skin. The gentle, almost reluctant, touch of his knuckles across her abs sent a shiver down her spine that had nothing to do with the cold.

That close and nothing. He'd kissed her like there was no tomorrow while stuck in that dug-out cage, igniting all sorts of warmth and emotions she should have set aside.

Now they were free and he'd only touched her to save her from the cactus. Okay, that was an exaggeration. He'd locked forearms with her to help her climb and kept her from falling several times.

The fight in the pool had been to obtain the knife. He'd risked his life and had given her the way out. "Are we going to talk about your heroics back at Bishop's?"

"Stick out your tongue."

"What?"

"I could use my spit, but you might think it's kind of gross." He gestured to her chin. "You've got a couple of spots."

She stuck out her tongue and he dabbed the piece of her shirt, then wiped at her chin, then the side of her nose and her forehead. Neither of them had cleaned up for two days, so she was definitely curious why wiping her face was important.

"I bet my entire face is dirty. Why—"

He showed her the makeshift rag. Blood from the man she'd fought and killed. She took the cloth, weaving her fingers through his while stuffing the rag in her coat pocket.

They'd each killed a man tonight and then had worked together to kill another. Bishop's men would have killed them. They'd tried. She wouldn't admit it, but she was upset and still shaky. Killing someone could eat up a good man. And Nick was one of the best she'd met.

"Are you all right with everything that happened?" How many times could she ask a grown man if he was okay? Maybe she wanted him to ask her for once.

"Why wouldn't I be? I've seen a dead man before. You were there. I didn't fall apart then."

"But you were angry when it happened." Beth felt the tug on her fingers but tugged back. "Do you want to talk about the guy in the front seat?"

"No." He looked off in the distance, but when his gaze darted back and landed on her, he'd search the darkness again. "I want to get my bearings and get us to a state campground along the border before Bishop's men come up behind us with guns blazing."

His fingers slid from hers as he stood and searched the horizon under the cloudy night sky as if he was lost. They could barely see in front of them with the blackness of night. He had to know where they were. "This is so not Chicago where there's a light on every street corner."

"Nope." He stuck his hands in his front pockets, pulling his elbows in close to his ribs, and continued scanning the perimeter. "No street lights."

"Nick?" Whatever landmark he was trying to find was a complete mystery to her. There was nothing. He had to be kidding around or plain old avoiding a conversation about their escape. "So, how are you going to determine where we are? It's pitch black out here."

"I know that the cold front was moving in from the northwest." He pointed. "The wind changes pretty quick out here, but there's a line of stars close to the horizon where the clouds have blown past. Their direction has been steady, so I can assume. I'm just trying to figure out where we are."

"Wait. You weren't joking a minute ago? I thought you knew exactly where we were. Isn't that what you said yesterday?"

He shrugged and smiled deeply. "So maybe I didn't have exact coordinates. Between the gully where we were held captive and this terrain, it looks a lot like what's south of Santa Elena Canyon. If we head there, we should be able to find someone with a cell phone. It's close to where people kayak. An outfitter puts in there. It's also on a scenic drive through the park, so it might have some early morning traffic."

When he looked tall, dark and handsome as he did right that very moment, it was too difficult to get upset with him. Besides, he'd been trying to reassure her, not deceive her.

"How far is it?" she said, extending a hand so he'd help her stand.

"Five, maybe seven miles of hard hiking. It'll take longer at night."

"All the way on foot..." The idea of walking that far wasn't at all appealing. "Isn't there a road where we could catch a ride? Scratch that. I know why we can't. That was the hunger talking."

"Look, Beth. This is going to be hard. Probably a lot harder than any workout you've gone through. I'd go alone, but there's no real place for you to hide around here. It's a good idea to get going again."

"How can you be so certain we'll get to where you're heading and not walk off a cliff?" Beth dusted herself off, desperately wanting to take off her boots instead of beginning a seven-mile hike.

"Lots of things, but mainly, there's a trail."

"This is a trail? I thought it was a goat path."

"More likely deer and javelinas. They come up here for the cactus. I'd rather mess with the cactus than one of those tusks. The path will lead us to water. Eventually. And that's what we want."

"Any chance we're near water now? Javelinas?" Asking what the animal was probably made her sound even more unprepared for her West Texas assignment, which was now in Mexico.

"Javelinas are wild pigs. This time of year they're mainly out in the mornings. If you're thirsty, give me the knife."

She was and she did. He knelt to where she'd been sitting, chopped some of the cactus apart, carefully and thoroughly scraped a few needles and handed it to her.

"Chew on that."

"Are you sure it's safe?"

"What? You've never eaten *nopalitos*?"

"Can't say that I have."

"Don't be such a snob. It's good for you, especially if you're thirsty." Nick sliced another huge leaf from the cactus behind her and used the blade to scrap the prickly parts. "We should get moving. Bishop's men are sure to be following on ATVs or horses. We won't have a lead for very long and need to cover as much ground as possible."

Even without its needles, the cactus seemed threatening. People really ate this? Was she a snob for not wanting to? Her stomach growled loud enough to make Nick chuckle. He broke his cactus in half, took a bite and smiled as he chewed.

It couldn't be as horrible as some of the things her parents had introduced her to while she'd grown up. When Beth had been fourteen, it had been one new weird edible a month while Elizabeth had been on a tangent. But they'd never gotten around to eating the garden plants.

The pale green skin was bumpy where the needles had been. Nick took another exaggerated bite as if it was the best meal he'd ever had. Or better yet, exactly as if it were one of his mother's biscuits.

"Come on, it really isn't that bad. Kind of tastes like green beans with lemon juice."

She nibbled. It was different, tart and weirdly edible. And he was right. It dampened her parched throat. But eating anything just made her rumbling stomach rumble louder. In turn, Nick laughed louder, drawing her attention to the long scar he couldn't stand for anyone to see.

"Aren't you cold?" she asked to change the subject.

"A bit."

"Take my jacket then."

"No."

"Don't be silly. It might be a tight fit, but it's warmer than nothing." She tried to shrug out of the coat, but he stopped her.

"It's more important that you stay warm. I can deal with it. Makes me walk faster. Don't worry so much." His chin dropped to his chest, just above the long scar on his breast bone.

When he glanced up his smile had been replaced with a somber, pragmatic look. "Beth, if something happens to me, you should know how to get out of here. Once the sun comes up, it'll be easy to see which direction is north. Just keep walking until you cross the river. Stay away from the roads unless you see a person you're certain you can trust."

"Turn around."

"What? Why?"

"Were you shot tonight? Is there an injury I don't know about?" She knew there wasn't, but didn't know what else to do. She couldn't think about Nick not being there to guide her out. Or that she'd let him down by not defending him.

"I don't know what you're talking about. I'm fine."

"Then let's get moving. Stop talking like you're going to disappear into this very thin desert mountain air. We're both getting back home. And believe me, we're calling your mom ahead of time so the biscuits will be ready." She pushed by him and made a grand exit from their scene, right up to the point where she realized she was walking back the direction they'd already come.

The six-foot-three Energizer Bunny hopped down the trail fresh and bouncy as if he'd just gotten up. He passed her on the slim path chewing on his cactus, leading the way north. She took another bite, not minding the tartness as much this time.

"You never did tell me how you know so much about this area. Aren't we a long way from Marfa?" She followed, matching his stride. "You don't run to these mountains on your day off. Or do you?"

"The park is about two hours from the town and you know how long it takes to get from town to the ranch. Actually, I minored in geology at Texas Tech, so I know a few things about the area. The Big Bend is a geological wonder."

"You know, there are a lot more layers to you than I originally thought, Nick Burke."

"Just goes to show you shouldn't make up your mind about a person before you know them."

Did he realize he spoke as much to himself as to her? He'd assumed a lot of things about her before he knew anything at all. "I don't think I assumed anything incorrectly. It was you who called me a greenhorn from Chicago."

"Which you are. And a foot model who's wearing purple boots. You have no business being in these mountains wearing rhinestones." He pointed to her new footwear.

"Wow. There's no reason to be snippy. I'll let it pass this time because I know you're cold. Don't deny it. I'm cold so you have to be freezing. All I asked was how you know this area."

"Fine. I was a guide here for a while and things didn't work out." He shoved his fingers through his hair and then rubbed his face like someone extremely nervous. Nervous as in someone discovering the truth. "Did you know there are at least four hundred and fifty species of birds in the park? It's more than any other national park in the States."

"Interesting, but come on. I told you about my short-lived modeling career and how much I love shoes."

"That's a little different than being the only child who will inherit a ranch but wanted to study rocks instead."

"But you chose the ranch. What's so wrong about exploring rocks in your spare time?" His look gave him away. "You didn't want to stay on the ranch. You wanted to leave and do something with rocks?"

"You wouldn't understand."

"Wait a minute." She grabbed his shoulder and he spun around. "What's that supposed to mean?"

"I wasn't dedicated to the cattle or running the ranch, before everything."

"Before the shooting?" Her gaze dropped to his chest. Nick ran his fist over the scar.

"That's right. Before the shooting I left the everyday details of my ranch in the hands of the man who wound up shooting me."

"There's nothing wrong—"

"Don't you get it? It's my fault. My own damn fault that I died. If I hadn't been fooling around, I might have discovered Mac's off-the-books activities."

"Or just been shot sooner. You can't play the what-if game, Nick. It'll drive you crazy if you do." She tried to comfort him, to touch him.

He yanked away, walking and hurling his next insult over his shoulder. "You can't possibly know what it's like."

"Seriously? Based on what exactly?"

"I didn't mean anything by it. No insult intended. I'm just all talked out." He threw up his hands and strode away, shuffling a little more than he had ten minutes earlier.

In the direction he'd pointed, she could see that more of the sky was clear. Now that the wind had picked up, the cloud cover had blown away. She noticed his movements were a little jerky or frustrated. His strength seemed to be ebbing, but he was determined to stay on his feet.

What had given him the impression that she wouldn't understand? Hadn't she already shared that her parents hadn't supported her decision not to follow in their footsteps? It was hard to follow him with the unwanted tears in her eyes. She thought they had something in common. That the experience of the last few days had brought them closer.

The past six months hit her. Hard. Out of the blue. Mistakes. Consequences. How much everyone wanted her to fail and how well she was succeeding at accommodating them.

Embarrassing as it was, it felt cleansing to let it out. Her cheeks were as wet as Nick's had been after he'd climbed from the pool. She couldn't get the tears to stop and for once, she didn't care. Her parents weren't around to see or tell her to grow up. She held in the sound until she hiccupped.

And hiccupped.

Nick ignored her, or at least he pretended not to notice. They walked up a small hill and down the other side. A path barely wide enough for one boot couldn't really pass for a trail. Right?

"Good grief, is there no flat trail to follow anywhere in West Texas?"

"Technically, this is Mexico until we cross the Rio Grande."

She let the smart-alecky remark pass. She wasn't in the mood yet for a real conversation. "How much farther?"

"You need a rest?"

"To be quite honest, I'm exhausted and it's getting harder to keep my feet from slipping on every small pebble in the way."

"Stay here. Let me check on something."

"Nick, don't—" But it was too late. She couldn't follow and wanted nothing more than to lie down where she was and sleep. The narrow path had no place to really rest. If she sat where she was she'd never get up on her own.

Stakeouts had never been this rough. If she could just close her eyes for a few minutes…

"Okay, let's go."

Beth jumped out of her skin at the sound of Nick's voice. Apparently she had closed her eyes and was lucky she hadn't fallen off the narrow path, down the steep slope.

"Were you asleep standing up?" he asked, steadying her shoulders and smiling for the first time since they'd eaten cactus. "Good thing I found us a place to rest awhile. It's right around the next turn."

They were both done in, but that didn't stop her next words from slipping from her lips. "I can keep going, but if you need to stop…"

With the raising of one eyebrow, he suggested her statement was ludicrous, which it was. "If I wasn't so beat up, I'd carry you around the bend. Afraid you're going to have to walk." He scooted her past him, put his hands on her waist and walked in sync with her.

"And here I thought you were my own personal superhero."

Chapter Sixteen

Nick wanted to lift Beth in his arms and play the hero. If it were up to his head, he'd carry her the remaining miles to the border. But it had taken everything in him to remain upright and get them this far from Bishop's camp. Half the reason he'd been able to stay awake was that he was cold, but that was working against him now. He was frozen to the bone and craving some shuteye himself.

A few feet farther and they'd be safe for awhile. Just a few feet farther...

He spotted a place to stop on the side of the slope. Only an indentation, but it would have to do. He pointed, but she stood there, eyes almost closed and looked about ready to pass out on her feet again. He grabbed her waist and guided her to their cover.

With his boot, he scooted the loose pebbles from where they would sit and then brought the brush up closer to pull on top of them. The wind had really picked up and the scrub would block some of it. At least the sky was clearing.

"Will Bishop's men catch us? I've sort of been expecting someone to start shooting for the last hour or so."

"They will eventually. Will they do it here? I'm not sure."

In no time at all, they were wrapped inside her coat,

arms and legs tangled. He was used to the way her body molded to his when it was close. *God, she's warm.*

"Good grief, you're an iceberg. All you need is a sharp point and you could rip the *Titanic* in two." Beth shivered, then began to briskly rub life into his arms.

"No sharp points on me. Yet." He tilted his head back and winked, receiving a tap to his chest when she finally got the crass implication. But she kept running her hands up and down his arms and over his chest.

The pain when she glided over his bruised ribs was worth it. Her hands had new calluses from working in the barn, but he didn't mind. Dirt from their captivity and their escape stained her fingers. The only reason his were clean-ish was because of the soak in the pool. She'd looked like a warrior standing up to Bishop and his men. Defending Nick and taking her job more seriously than he'd thought possible when they'd first met a month ago.

He'd been an ass back then. Complaining about her lack of horse skills, about her attitude, when all along it had been a simple case of fright. As scared as she was, she'd never cried about it. So what was different this time?

"Why were you crying?"

"I wasn't. Totally your imagination. And if I was, it's none of your business."

"Beth." He took her chin between his fingers and tilted it toward his. "I couldn't stop and ask what was wrong earlier. But I'm asking now."

"I'm just tired."

"And you're lying." He rubbed at her cheeks, smearing the evidence of tear trails. "Come on, you know all my deepest darkest nightmares."

"I told you mine."

"That you were a foot model. Right. But that's not the reason you were sent to West Texas." With the first rays of sunshine coming over the hill, he could finally see her brilliant eyes as they clouded over in sadness.

"Oh, when everyone found out, it was absolutely brutal." She attempted to shrug it off. "I probably should have told you when I first moved in, but the time never seemed right."

"It couldn't be worse than the past two days."

"It depends on what happens if we finally make it to the border."

"*When* we make it to the border. The river's just over that ridge. Hard to see from here, but it is." Pressed against her, wrapped in her arms, he was warm and relaxed for the first time since they'd made love two days ago. He wanted to encourage her to share. "Tell me."

"You're right. I messed up and was sent here to fail."

"What happened?"

A long sigh, followed by some shifting away from him, then another long sigh, and Nick scooted her back into the crook of his arms. Avoidance. He recognized it and had become an expert at it in the past year. But she hadn't given up on him and he wouldn't just forget about her crying.

"You aren't going to let this go, are you? Is it payback for me prying into your nightmares?"

"Nope. More like, I want to know why you were crying, and sort of hoping it wasn't because of me."

"Well, it was, in the beginning. I wanted to be there in case you needed to talk about the men dying and it made me remember. I do every day—remember, that is—but then it sort of hit me and it all came bubbling to the surface."

They needed rest, sleep. Not to dredge up memories of why she'd been sent there to fail. He pulled her in tight and held on. There'd be plenty of time to talk after this was over. He didn't know what had come over him, insisting that she talk. Maybe it was because he was curious or felt guilty for ignoring her crying earlier. It wasn't—couldn't be—because he was in love with her.

Damn. It had already happened. There was no use trying to ignore it. He was head over heels for Beth Conrad. Somewhere between teaching her to ride a horse and flipping her into the hay during defense training, he'd slipped from attraction to caring. Definitely before they'd made love in the cabin, and then more since they'd spent two days in a hole where she hadn't complained.

"Never mind. Let's grab some rest while we can. Close your eyes, hon." He hugged her as reassuringly as he could.

They'd been walking all night and his brain was foggier than it had been in a long time. He couldn't remember what they'd been talking about or even if they'd had an argument. Sad, but true. He was just that plain tired.

"Your country is pretty, but it's such a dangerous and desolate place. I'd rather be on the beach. Where do you want to be?"

He followed her line of sight into the small valley. The last vestiges of the stars were disappearing as the sun peaked fully over the hills. He pressed his lips against her hair before he remembered he probably shouldn't. Hell, why shouldn't he?

"Other than having you safe, why would I want to be anywhere else? I'm watching the sunrise with my girl."

And that's what he got for having a conversation when he was so blasted tired. Even though he meant to show his concern, he shouldn't have brought it up now.

"I'm your girl?" She turned her beautiful, dirt-smudged face toward his.

"You aren't?" He didn't have a clue what to say next. She hid her face again and he wondered if his face reflected his surprise.

"I thought we were just having some fun while you waited out my assignment," she said into the coat covering his shoulder.

"Yeah, I suppose you're right. Thanks for setting me straight." What the heck? She was a woman, right? Didn't they want commitments? To her credit, she'd never asked for one. Never hinted at anything more than a good time.

"That's not what I meant."

"I don't think you left much room for interpretation." It was his turn to shift, trying to put a couple of inches between them.

"Oh, no you don't. I am freezing half to death. You don't have a shirt on. I can feel how cold you are, so get yourself as close as possible and huddle for warmth." She rubbed her palms up and down his back, keeping him in place next to her. "I can't believe I'm wishing to be all tangled up with you again like back in that horrible cave. But I am. It was warmer there."

"Clouds are gone. It'll be warmer once the sun's fully up. No snow for a while." He was not returning to the bungled question about her being his girlfriend. Enough was enough. A guy's ego could only take so much.

"There's really nothing around as far as you can see, is there? Are you certain we're heading toward civilization?"

"No reason to worry. We've been mirroring the main trail most of the night."

She pulled back and gave him a sharp, questioning look. "Are you saying there's a better, easier path down there? One that might have been quicker?"

"Sure, but it would be quicker for Bishop's men, too."

She covered her face with both hands. "I should be able to think of that. I know things like that. Why can't I think and say what I mean? I need to clarify why you surprised me a minute ago." She yawned big, letting out a sleepy sigh.

"Close your eyes, Beth," he said a second time, encouraging her to lay her head on his shoulder. "Neither one of us can think straight when we're this tired."

"But you asked why I was crying and I should tell you," she paused, yawned deeply. "An agent died because I... hesitated. They couldn't fire me, so they sent me here. I just want to—" she yawned again "—to get...home..."

Seconds later she was deep asleep.

Hesitated? Then that was the real reason she'd been so fast to protect him. He couldn't fault her for that. He'd do the same. Had done it last night in order to escape.

Nick supported his head on Beth's and closed his eyes. They were taking a risk with both of them asleep. But without rest they'd be unable to function, especially if Bishop's men found them. He'd taken every precaution that he could. They wouldn't be spotted from the air because of the slight rock overhang. It would be difficult to see them from a distance with the brush in front of them. And they were off the main trail, so no one would stumble over them.

He'd done everything he could to protect Beth.

He wished he'd done more to protect his heart. Just his luck that he'd fallen in love with a woman who was totally unavailable. Beth said she wanted to go home, but she hadn't been talking about the Rocking B.

BETH SEARCHED FOR the edge of the covers, wanting to pull them closer around her neck and cut the chill. A few more minutes and she was certain the alarm would sound. She'd really like to cover her head and finish the intoxicating dream she'd been having about Nick.

Nick?

The faint stinging smell of chlorine forced her to blink herself awake and away from the heady images swirling around in her vision. She stayed put, wanting to remember the musky, earthy smell that was the man still in her arms. His skin might be masked with a stringent chemical, but she'd never forget the way her body chose to remember his.

Speckles of sunshine drifted through the leaves across them both. A new day. A new chance to make things right. She'd flubbed their last conversation terribly. She couldn't really blame it on exhaustion—though she would until her dying breath. The whole thing had just taken her by such surprise.

I'm watching the sunrise with my girl.

Maybe he'd been exhausted and hadn't meant to say it. No, that was the woman in her, trying to make an excuse for how badly she'd reacted. He'd meant to say it. In fact, he'd repeated it and almost seemed hurt that she hadn't thought about it.

Quite the contrary. She hadn't allowed herself to think about it. From the moment she'd asked him for permission to stay on his ranch, she'd forced herself to think of it as an assignment. Not a relationship.

Each time his father taught her something about the garden or even mucking a stall, she'd swallowed hard and pushed her feelings aside. So, yes, she'd been surprised by his admission. And now she needed a clear head to think about it. And to think about the consequences their current adventure would have on her career.

If she still had a career with the DEA. But first things first. They still needed to get back to civilization.

The branches at the edge of their makeshift enclosure wiggled. Beth slowly drew up her leg, bending it so that her thigh pinned Nick's arm between them.

"Wake up, Nick," she whispered urgently but as softly as she could into his ear.

Whatever was rustling the branches was getting closer. Beth's first thought had been that Bishop's men had found them. But if those movements were human, it was the quietest human on the face of the planet. So it had to be a small animal.

What if it was one of those wild javelina things he'd mentioned? All he'd said was that she didn't want to mess with one. She hated to wake him, but just in case it wasn't something that could be scared away with a shout, she placed her finger across his lips. "Nick?"

His eyes popped open and darted back and forth. There was no question that he remembered where they were. She felt his hand tighten around the hilt of the knife she'd been attempting to ease from his fingers.

"Something's getting close." She moved her hand to his shoulder.

"Get behind me," he whispered.

The space was bigger than their cave so it wasn't nearly as hard to switch positions as it had been for the past two days. The trick was being quiet about it. Nick crouched at the opening of the shelter and listened. The rustling was closer. She could see the branch nearest to Nick moving.

"It's just a blue quail." He rolled back and sat. "You really had my heart pumping for a minute."

"What a relief." Her stomach growled, interrupting whatever thought she was about to share as the bird got startled and flew away. "Do you think there's more cactus availa—"

Nick's hand in her face cut her off. She listened for movement as intently as her partner. The faint sound of pebbles peppering against other rocks grew louder.

That wasn't an animal sound. It was boots scuffing rock. Footsteps. It was Bishop's men.

Knife in hand, Nick shook his head, painstakingly retreating nearer to her in amazing silence. An electronic ping of a cell phone split the void. Neither she nor Nick moved or even twitched. No one walked on the path in front of them. No one answered the cell and no one stuck a gun in their face.

Her muscles had ached before this. Now the faint beginnings of another cramp was about to seize her calf. If she pointed her toe, she'd stretch into the branches hiding them and give away their location.

She tapped on Nick's bare shoulder, pointed to her leg, then cupped her hand over her mouth. He shifted the knife to his left hand and firmly gripped her calf and massaged it, relaxing the tense muscle. She kept her eyes wide, waiting for their intruder to find them. Nick asked her silently if her leg was okay, and she nodded. Then her stomach growled. A ginormous roar that put a priceless look on the cattleman's face. At any other time she would have snapped a picture and used it for social-media fun.

But not now.

Please be gone. Please be gone. Please be gone. They needed a break.

They waited several more minutes. Nick was at the ready to defend her and she'd be right behind him doing her part. They made a good team. She decided then that as soon as the opportunity came up, she'd talk to him about being "his girl."

"The quail's back. I don't think anyone's out there now. Ready to get going? We'll keep it quiet, stay close to any juniper you see. Does that coat have metal?" He turned toward her, using the knife to slice all the buttons and drop them to the dirt. "With the sun out today, we don't want any reflections drawing attention to our location."

"You know, you're pretty good at this, Nick Burke."

"I watch a lot of Westerns."

His smile tugged on her heartstrings. She wanted to set the record straight about their relationship right then, but they didn't have the time. And if she kissed him instead…?

Wrong place. Wrong time.

"Give me a sec to take a look around." He left, putting the cut branches back in place to hide her.

Feeling helpless wasn't her style. She'd had a plan since junior high when writing a paper on possible careers. She'd chosen the DEA. She'd mapped out her plan, argued with her parents, put herself through school totally confident in her choice the entire time. She'd put up with the discriminating remarks because she was a woman. They had made her tougher. And she'd helped capture and put away criminals she never wanted to think about again.

So why did walking next to a hot cowboy make her all gaga? She'd dated in Chicago—at least every once in a while.

She stretched her tired arms and legs. How long should she wait? He hadn't said.

No permission was needed. She was a trained agent. She could make her own decisions. She was scooting forward when Nick cleared the opening and helped her stand.

"No one's in sight. Beth, I wanted you to know that I'm sorry for bringing Bishop down on you."

"Oh, my— You thought that getting caught by Bishop would give you answers, didn't you? Did you get them? Putting both our lives at risk that way? What if they'd just shot us and been done with it? How would you have said you're sorry then?"

"That's not it. I'd never… Think whatever you want."

He pointed to the north. "You'll be able to see the river in no time. Once you're there, head into the sun and you should run into someone who doesn't work for Bishop."

"You're talking like you won't be there, too."

"I found their tracks, and I'm doubling back. I'll take the men following us by surprise. Maybe take a gun or a phone. They won't know what hit them."

"Alone? How will you hit them? With sticks and stones? They have the weapons, not us." She couldn't let him do it. "I can't believe you expect me to just let you go back on your own. You do remember that *I'm* the one that carries a damn badge and gun, right?"

"I did not forget." He rubbed his face and she thought he rolled his eyes.

It didn't matter. It wasn't a smart move and he needed to accept it. "What do you hope to gain?"

"A phone."

"That's ridiculous. We can't face them without backup. How close are we to the kayak place?"

He crossed his arms. "As tired as we are? Another hour or two. There's no guarantee that someone's there."

"So we'll break in. There will be no doubling back. No throwing sticks or stones. No debate. Yes, call me any name you want. It won't change my mind. We're going to find a way back to Marfa and take Bishop down."

The DEA agent was back issuing orders and this time she knew which direction to head as she walked away.

Chapter Seventeen

"I'm sure I can pick out the location of Bishop's compound from satellite photos, sir. And I have a working theory how to find the inside man at the Rocking B— Yes, sir. I know that avenue was pursued, but— Yes, sir, I did hear you that the investigation is closed. But regarding the shooting, if I may explain my reasons..."

Nick turned from the hallway where he'd been listening through the open door for a good half hour. Each time Beth began to explain to her superiors what had happened, they cut her off. Each time she began to lay out a plan, they cut her off. She was getting nowhere with the DEA and he was ready to get home.

He'd spoken to his mom and dad on the way to the hospital in Alpine. He convinced them that driving two hours to the hospital wasn't necessary and had thought he'd be home before they could make the trip. That was before he'd remembered that government bureaucracy was involved. Nothing went fast with that around.

Two cracked ribs, a hairline fracture across his nose, they'd finally made it to the sheriff's office in Marfa— more than half a day later.

Official statements. More questions. Diagrams. Shoot, they'd even gotten a sketch artist from Austin to work with him over a webcam. The one thing they hadn't asked him about was getting home. They were too concerned with capturing Bishop and blocking his next move.

No one showed signs of heading in the direction of the ranch anytime soon. Beth looked his way every few minutes while he grew impatient. His statement had been taken and he was done. At least he assumed he was. Mc-Crea had asked him to wait in the sheriff's personal office. After pacing those short four walls and then the length of the hallway avoiding Beth's call, he finally landed out front at reception.

"Mind if I use the phone, Miss Honey?"

Everyone called her Honey and called her sister Peach. The dispatchers insisted their nicknames were better than Wilhelmina and Winafretta.

"There's one in the empty office behind you, Nick," said the older receptionist who did double duty as a dispatcher.

"Thanks."

"You giving up on them and want a ride home?" she asked.

"Yes, ma'am." He wrapped his arm close to his side, holding the sore ribs. "I'm about all done in."

"Your parents will be glad to have you home safe."

He'd been expecting to hear from them for a while now. Wishing they would barge in like when he was a teenager and had driven to Alpine to buy beer using a fake ID. That trip they'd left him in jail overnight to teach him a lesson. Pete's dad had been sheriff at the time and had made Nick clean the building for a month.

"I'm surprised mom hasn't been calling every half hour."

"Who says she hasn't?" Honey laughed and waved him toward the empty office. "Would you like me to tell them you need a ride after all? I don't blame you for wanting some peace and quiet. It's been a regular circus around here for a good while now. You hungry? I'm taking an order for the café."

"No, thanks. We ate right before we got here." His stomach was starting to grumble. Not as loudly as Beth's had a tendency to do.

"That was three hours ago. You sure? I heard you two went without food for a while. And, Nick Burke, you are already skin and bones. You need to put some meat back on that tall frame of yours."

"Yes, ma'am. Thanks, anyway, but I think mom made us a pan of biscuits." He took another step closer to the phone. Maybe, if he was lucky, he'd catch one of the hands still at the house.

"Your momma sure does know how to make biscuits. You should think twice before you run off again, young man. Okay? Your daddy said your momma was worried sick. Of course she said the same thing about him. They practically lived online while you were missing."

"Online? What do you mean?" He moved closer to Honey's desk, away from the old sheriff's office and Beth's conversation.

"They were emailing and chatting with people to see if there was any sign or news of you. I did what I could, but as you know, we didn't have any idea where you'd been taken."

"I, um…" He'd spent so little time at the house during the day that he had no clue how his parents used their time. "I never pictured my mom and dad hanging out anywhere, especially online."

"Oh, yeah. Your dad cracks me up with some of the stories from his buds in his support group," Beth said coming up behind him.

"Do you have a way out of here yet?" he asked.

"Sure. I just got some keys from Pete." She moved to his

side and dangled them in front of him like a shiny fish lure. "He's loaning me a service vehicle to pick up my stuff."

"'Night, Honey."

"Take care of yourself. If not for you, then do it for your mother."

"Yes, ma'am."

Being treated like a teenager didn't bother him. He might be thirty years old, but this was Marfa. He'd worried his parents by taking off like a child. It didn't matter that the reason had seemed legitimate. There were other ways to deal with the situation. As several people in his life—and some on the internet—had suggested, it was time to seek out professional help to get rid of the nightmares.

Beth led the way through the halls of the county building. He followed her through the solid door into another clear night. She clicked the set of keys and headlights flashed across a sea of white Tahoes.

Nick snatched the keys from her fingers. "You drive like a maniac. No way am I letting you drive us home."

"But this is an official Sheriff's Department vehicle."

"I promise to drive it like a regular Tahoe and not sound the siren." He quickened his steps just in case she tried to take the keys back. She probably could drop him on the pavement before he knew what had hit him.

"Oh, I'm fairly certain that you have no intention of keeping that promise. Do you?"

"Nope." He turned the key, got the engine going, but took a minute to look at all the extras the county vehicle sported.

"Did I hear you tell Honey— By the way, it is so hard to call a grown woman that. It makes me feel silly."

"Tell her what?" They were officially out of Marfa and on their way home.

She yawned. "Guess I'm a little more tired than I

thought. Anyway, did you tell Honey that your mom had made biscuits? My taste buds are watering just thinking of the possibility."

"Mom said she would this afternoon. You know, I can't remember the last time we had leftover biscuits. They never last that long around her kitchen."

"Stop, stop, stop. You're making me hungrier." She laughed.

"You, um, planning on driving back to Marfa tonight?" he asked, trying not to sound too concerned. He wasn't certain how he felt about that. He'd spent the past couple of hours wondering how he would get into her room without being heard by his parents or sneak them both to the hayloft in the barn. He hadn't really given much time to how he would stay away.

"No. I've been ordered back to Chicago."

Now he didn't have to wonder about it. She was leaving. He couldn't open his mouth and ask her to stay. She had a job. She had a life. One that didn't include him.

"The key word here, Nick, is *ordered*. It's not like I want to return before this case is finished. But it's not my decision."

"You'd be going back eventually."

"That's true. But I want to find the man spying on your ranch for Bishop. I want to take Bishop down. Every time I think about what he did to you… He's a monster and I want to be the one to stop him."

"Weren't you just reminded that there is no spy or informant?" He'd surely been reminded of it enough by Pete.

"There has to be. Someone is telling Bishop about your movements."

"I don't know, Beth. You haven't been around the men or their families like I have. Some of them I've known for over a decade. Who would you choose?"

His gut had been telling him there was more to his shooting, screaming at him not to trust a soul on his ranch and maybe only a few in town.

She buried her face in her hands, her ebony hair creating a curtain between them. "I don't know. None of them, really. They've all been so kind." She shoved her hair back, unconsciously fluffing it into place. A gesture that he'd come to expect and enjoy.

He didn't want her to go. It hit him so hard that he gripped the wheel too tightly and caused the Tahoe to swerve.

"You okay?"

"Yeah, just thinking." Thinking that it had been an intense month of a friendship or a relationship. And she was preparing to gather her things and leave.

"Oh, my gosh, what if it's not anyone who works at the ranch at all?"

"I don't follow. No one's believed there is an informant, so you're finally agreeing with them?"

"I think it's your parents. By accident of course."

"Now hold on a minute—"

"They're online, Nick. Don't you get it? It's someone they think to be their friend online. Bishop could be discussing recipes with your mom or pretending to be someone with cancer in your father's support group."

Nick turned off the main road, heading across the half mile to the house. "What do we do if it is? How do we catch someone who technically doesn't exist?"

"Don't discount that it may be a real person. Mac was in it for the money, and someone else could be, too. Several ranchers and their wives are talking to your parents. You heard Honey back at the station. Everybody knew how worried your parents were."

"It might be spread out, but it's basically a small town.

You don't have to be on the internet to know what's going on. It's not Chicago."

"*Hmph.* Don't I know it."

He didn't look at her. He couldn't. She was leaving and he had to face that fact. Get over it fast. If he wanted her help, he had to accept that their relationship wasn't going to move to the next level. He should be used to that.

Stop brooding like an old hen and find the traitor.

"We need to find the informant without alerting him that we're looking," Beth said. "Thing is, I'm off the task force and I've been ordered back to Chicago, so I won't be much help from there. Promise me you'll stay close to the ranch until they find Bishop. Remember that he wants you dead."

"We can use that to our advantage. If I don't leave the ranch, he'll have to send someone there to finish me off."

"Don't talk like that. But you're right. I'd feel more comfortable if you had a protective detail—"

"No. We know the task force doesn't believe there's a threat."

He pulled in front of the house. The headlights passed across his parents sitting on the porch swing. His dad stood, gripped the column, waiting. Nick could see the tension in his father's face. When had he gotten so haggard? All through the chemo he'd been feisty. Tired, but as ornery as usual.

"Then who's going to help you, Nick? And don't say you don't need it. Someone has to watch your back, and you need help going through the hundreds of online friends your parents have."

Bishop wanted him dead and he was using an informant to get the information to do it. What would happen to his parents then? How haggard would his dad be the next time? That was *if* he returned after a next time.

"Stay."

"I'd need a legitimate reason that doesn't concern this case. You should know—"

"You could marry me."

"What?" Her long, loose hair whipped around her like a fan as she faced him so quickly.

"We can turn the first fake engagement that everyone knew about into a real fake engagement that only a few people know about." Then she'd be around for a while longer, which would be fine by him.

"Do you think it would work? You'd really have to play it up to make everyone believe it."

"Not a problem." He wouldn't be acting. He'd be convincing her to stay. "What about your job?"

"I'd like to finish this assignment. I…I could arrange for some leave." Filtered light from the porch lit her face through the windshield, exposing a moment of sadness. She had to be worried about keeping her job if they found out.

"If you can take time off from your job, I can promise to stay put on the ranch."

"Excellent. But if you want this to work, absolutely no one can know it's fake. Especially not your parents."

Guess she wasn't heading back to Chicago after all.

NICK WRAPPED HIS long fingers around Beth's shoulders, pulling her to the middle of the Tahoe. The clean jacket someone had given her after the hospital caught on the seat belt, preventing her from getting closer. She couldn't look away from the power he radiated. Whatever he'd intended to say, it looked to be important.

"You know what you're asking? You want me to lie to my parents and have them lie to whoever they talk to. But I'm willing to do that, Beth. Very willing if you tell me how we reach the end game and ferret out the weasel taking advantage of them. And—" His voice raised a little, but he caught himself and spoke normally again. "And if you do find this guy, I don't want my parents to know they may have been responsible for getting us abducted."

She cupped his whiskered jaw. Her fingertips drew little circles where they landed. She'd been wanting to touch him since they'd been picked up that morning. Especially now when he seemed so vulnerable for once. "That's a sweet thought, Nick, but you have extremely intelligent parents. Don't you think they'll become angrier if they're kept in the dark? Besides, they need to be more careful with the information they put out there. Even to friends."

"I suppose you're right."

Did he know he'd turned his cheek into her hand? Or that his brown eyes had softened and grown sad for his parents? The bandage strips and bruises around his nose didn't detract from how handsome he was. The wretched man who had ordered Nick's beatings had to be caught before he ordered Nick's death again.

"We better get out of the car. My dad's on the steps now. Another minute and he'll be jerking me out of here by my collar. And I'm not even wearing one."

Nick looked sexy in the hospital scrub top he'd been given. He'd insisted on keeping his jeans. She'd heard him in the emergency room arguing that he could stand up and take them off himself.

"I'll tell the task force. They'll be the only ones who know the truth. Between the four of us, we can find this guy."

"Wait. No. No one means just us, no one else." He shook his head, pressing his lips together stubbornly. "If we do this, then it's just you and me."

"But I never meant to exclude them. We have new evidence—"

"Did your boss listen to that new theory? We don't have evidence. Pete and Cord's hands are tied by men who don't live here, Beth. The people making the decisions aren't the ones who have anything to risk or who will catch the bullet that's fired into their back."

"Maybe if I get another agent to work with you? My supervisor doesn't receive any suggestion I make." *Tell him.*

He should know that she'd been ordered to return to Chicago and subsequently would be placed on disciplinary leave for her mistakes of the past months. Her supervisor had been anxiously awaiting for her failure here. She'd succeeded in making a fool of herself more than once. Being abducted by Bishop and endangering a citizen was just the ammunition they needed.

"It's too late for that. I know what you're risking. You could lose everything. I get that. Staying and helping will get you into a lot of trouble. But I have to do it this way. It's just you and me or we don't have a deal."

"We need the task force's help, its resources. Working on our own will be impossible."

The opportunity to tell him was slipping away with every millimeter Nick moved backward. She had to be honest with him. She was on her way out of the DEA. If she informed McCrea of their plan, there was no guarantee he'd listen to her, either.

Nick shrugged. It was her decision.

"There's something you should know—"

The door opened behind her and she sat straight in her seat. "You kids going to get out? We won't yell. Much." Alan and Juliet were ready to see their son.

"Oh, don't be silly, Alan. Of course we're not going to yell. Come on inside and tell us all about it. Or don't say a word. Your choice." She stepped in front of Alan, who still held the door. "Go help Nick, hon. I've got Beth."

Juliet hid her reaction to their bruises well. Alan inhaled sharply but also held his tongue.

"I'm okay, really." She heard the same words behind her as Nick spoke to his dad. But they went unheard. The broken nose had been set, but his black eyes emphasized his pain.

The Burkes took their elbows and led them up the steps as if they were a hundred years old. Nick quirked an eyebrow and winked at her, playing along. Juliet sniffled and knuckled away a tear. Beth could only imagine how it felt to see your only child beat up and lucky to be alive.

Again.

There was more at stake than just finding an informant. She'd tried to make her commander in Chicago understand that Bishop wanted Nick dead.

Nick's words rang true. *The people making the decisions aren't the ones who have anything to risk or who will catch the bullet that's fired into their back.* She could take matters into her own hands, possibly go to jail as a result. Bishop needed to be caught. The informant needed to be caught.

The Burke family gathered at the kitchen table to eat homemade biscuits and jam. They didn't have anyone on their side. No one believed they were in danger. Except her.

She sat down across the table from Nick. Juliet had several meals laid out on the hand-embroidered tablecloth that matched more than one of her aprons.

"I can heat up whatever you'd like to eat whenever you're hungry. I left two servings in separate plastic containers," Juliet said nervously, joining them at the table. "If you want coffee I can make a pot."

"No, thanks," they answered together.

"Well, I figured you probably had enough coffee all day long and wouldn't need any this late."

"She threw out the last fresh pot about thirty minutes ago," Alan shared. "Wouldn't let me have a drop."

"I am so sorry." The words spilled from her faster than pop from a shaken bottle. "I couldn't keep your son safe."

Everyone spoke at once.

"It wasn't your fault," Juliet said, patting Beth's arm.

"Don't cry about it now. You're both all right." Alan squeezed her hand.

"What the hell?" Nick pushed away from the table, his mouth full of a biscuit. He swallowed. Everyone stared at him. "I didn't need protecting."

He glared at her. Eyes black instead of a soft warm brown. The bruising accentuated his glare.

"Don't get your knickers in a knot. Sit down and eat another biscuit," his mother said, pointing to his chair. "Sit."

"I didn't mean it that way, Nick. I would never have escaped if it hadn't been for you." She turned first to his mom and then his dad, then back to the man who'd grown to mean so much to her. As sincerely as she could, because she wanted him to know she meant it. Her explanation wasn't part of their ploy. "Your son saved my life."

Juliet's hand pressed over her heart. She sniffed again while Alan sat a little straighter in his chair. Beth reached across the table, laced her fingers in the reluctant grasp of Nick's and raced forward to tell them before she could change her mind.

No matter the consequences that would come later, she owed this man her life. She needed to be the person to keep that red sniper dot off his back. "Do you want to tell them, sweetheart?"

"Sweetheart?" Alan questioned.

Fortunately, his son wasn't taken by surprise. Maybe

her death grip on his hand had given him a warning. Realization dawned and his face softened from hurt pride to a look that was pure let's jump into this thing with both feet.

"I asked Beth to marry me for real," he said. "She's not going back to Chicago."

Stunned silence.

Then chaos.

Lots of hugs and more tears from Juliet. Alan uncorked a bottle of wine, insisting on toasting the happy couple. Nick held his ribs as he reached over his mother, getting four rarely used wineglasses from a top shelf.

"Carroll and Elizabeth have a rack of glasses over a wine bar they had installed last year. They love wine tastings." She held her glass, feeling the moment of awkwardness. The room had grown so silent she could hear the *glug-glug-glug* of wine being poured.

"Do you think your parents could come visit, dear?" Juliet asked while a smidgen of merlot was poured for her.

Her parents? She had no intention of telling them about this charade. "I'm sure they will, but there's no rush."

"There is if we throw an engagement party," Alan tossed out on cue.

Nick was no help. He looked as if he was watching a red dot shine on his heart. Actually, he looked more frightened at the prospect of meeting her parents than he had facing down Bishop.

"They don't travel much and I'm sure they're far too busy with end of semester grades and things." She'd explain to Nick later that she wouldn't really ask them.

"We'll work out all the details tomorrow. For right now, here's to Nick and Beth." Four glasses clinked together. "If you experience as much love in your lifetime together as I have in one minute with Juliet, you will surely be blessed."

It was a beautiful toast. She hated lying to them. Yet it

was a necessary evil. She sipped the merlot, wanting to gulp it down at the thought of how Nick's parents were going to react when they learned the truth. Once their son was safe and their family secure, she hoped they could forgive her.

Chapter Eighteen

"Checkmate." Bishop had played his latest game against himself so it was difficult to take much glory in the victory.

He rolled the black king between his palms, looking around the room at the things he'd come to think of as his. But they weren't. He'd been at this hacienda longer than any other and had grown accustomed to its comforts in spite of its remote location. Not much would be packed and taken to his next house.

Even the chess boards would stay here.

Resetting the intricately carved pieces for another round, he was interrupted by a timid knock and forced to change the direction of his thinking. He clenched the white rook. If he hadn't valued and respected the craftsmanship so much, he'd throw the piece into the bookcases.

One game would go unfinished. Its pieces had grown dusty since his stupid-ass opponent had been caught so easily by the Americans while trying to get their guns into Mexico. Everything about that plan had seemed a bit off.

The knock repeated. Time for someone to answer for the mistakes that had taken place recently.

"Enter," he said loud enough to be heard through the thick, dark mahogany. He would miss this study, the desk, the extensive library.

"You wanted to see me, Mr. Bishop? Did you need something?"

"Follow me." He led the way through the French doors to the dimly lit patio. The unsuspecting dolt was in step behind him, repeating the movements Burke had taken the previous day.

"I heard on the news that Burke was rescued and returned home safe and sound," Bishop said, faking a smile and obtaining the look of fear he'd wanted.

"We kept looking, just like you told us."

"Fool! I told you to find them, not let them escape! This phase should be completed by now. I should have taken care of Burke myself and not have delayed the final outcome." He removed the .44 Magnum from his tight belt, pointing and firing before the slug of a man had a chance to flee.

The body fell into the pool, the splash mixed with the slight spray of blood that had landed on his extended arm.

"Bravo," Patrice said behind him, clapping. "We're shorthanded and you choose to get rid of another warm body."

"Incompetent. He let them escape not once, but twice."

"Aw, you're angry because we're moving the operation and you won't have a hot tub. I know you've enjoyed it here. Maybe it's for the best, before you grow overly possessive." She laughed, picked up a towel and dropped it over his shoulder.

She twirled around him, dragging one sharp fingernail across his chest and around to his shoulders, smiling up at him as she passed and then staring into the ripples of the pool. The water turned pink as the body settled on the bottom with a face completely unrecognizable from the force of the bullet. Bishop enjoyed his Clint Eastwood gun and the damage it could do.

He slowly wiped the splatter of blood from his arms.

"Wanna jump in the hot tub one last time?" Patrice asked coyly.

Couldn't she see the diluted blood in the pool? It wasn't something he wanted covering his body. He pulled Patrice into his arms, capturing her tightly around her waist, allowing her to feel the desire his rash actions had elicited. After a hard kiss, her red lips slashed across his, he released her and turned them back toward the house.

"Why are you here, Patrice? Did they send you to oversee us abandoning this place? Are you, of all people, supposed to make certain we leave no evidence behind? I think we can handle the move."

Her eyes narrowed to small slits. The smile vanished for the briefest of moments before she flashed her nauseatingly white teeth at him again. "I'm supposed to make sure you leave the silver."

"There's little left to do. Report that."

"Excuse me, *senor*, but there is a phone call." The houseboy hung back, half in the doorway and half behind the glass door, cell in hand.

Bishop gestured for the boy to approach, then snatched the phone. The number was blocked, but he suspected who it was. "Yes?"

"I'm out. We're done."

"But we are not. I need your help again."

"You never said you'd be kidnapping anybody. I can't do things like that."

"Quit panicking and playing the martyr. You need money. I have money. It's a simple business transaction."

"Nick Burke could have been killed. I can't be responsible for somethin' like that."

He should have been killed! The man should have died several times over!

"Burke is the bane of my existence. If he isn't hurt, someone else will be. Think of your family."

"Yes, think of your family," Patrice repeated in a whisper.

While the informant babbled on the other end of the line, his blonde friend lounged in a nearby chair, smiling in a way he'd never seen before. It was the closest thing to evil he'd experienced. Her words rang in his ears, having nothing to do with threatening the informant.

She threatened him? His family? He'd proven his loyalty several times over, yet after all this time she'd been sent to remind him that the lives of his parents were in the hands of someone else?

"How am I supposed to go to the engagement party and look them in the eye? You know if I don't they'll be suspicious. So I think I better quit."

Engagement party?

"What party is this?" He turned his back to Patrice, wondering if a knife would be thrust into it soon.

"Haven't you been listening?" the voice whined. "Nick and that agent gal are getting married. His parents are throwing a surprise party next Saturday. The whole county's coming."

"Details." He growled the word, losing his patience with the fool.

"Um…we're supposed to show up around dusk. No gifts necessary."

Bishop disconnected the call and spun around to face Patrice. A very topless Patrice. Her red silky blouse and bra were open, her nipples rock hard because of the cold.

"Baby, I think you got the wrong impression why I'm here." The fingertips that had almost clawed him moments before drew concentric circles on the two silicon globes.

He didn't care. Just looking at her had him unbuckling his belt.

He straddled the lounge chair, ready to drop his face into her cool flesh, when a red nail poked him in the chest.

"Did you think of a way to get rid of Burke?"

"We can get rid of the entire task force, actually. They'll all be together at an engagement party. With the right supplies it won't be a problem." He leaned closer, her tanned flesh inches from his mouth.

Patrice's nail caught his bottom lip, stopping his descent. "It might be a good idea if you took care of the Burke problem yourself. I don't know how many more mistakes will be forgiven without consequences."

"You mean go to the ranch myself? But they know what I look like. How will I get close to them?"

She lifted her hips to his. "I'm sure you'll find a way."

"That's suicide."

"Well, sweetie." She sank her nails into his flesh. "There's always the alternative."

Death. Decapitation. His body rotting in the Mexican desert.

He wasn't a man who enjoyed public displays, yet his relationship with Patrice was laced with them. He was about to give her exactly what she wanted when the side gate opened and two of his men entered.

One of them nodded toward the pool. "They said for us to clean up out here, boss."

"No. Leave the incompetent fool for the *Federales*." It would give them something to do while he crashed an engagement party.

Chapter Nineteen

Nick greeted as many guests as he could. He wanted to look each of them in the eyes. If one of them couldn't meet his stare straight on, they'd move to the top of his suspect list.

But the crowd got thick real fast. Soon, he was grabbing trays and doing the bidding of his mother, unable to greet visitors at the door. He'd grown up with his mom and dad hosting a ton of get-togethers, but not since his father had first been diagnosed. Everyone in the county seemed to have shown up. Mainly to see the gal Nick Burke had "finally landed," as most of them put it.

People were shoulder to shoulder in every main room of the house. There was a poker game in full swing in the bunkhouse—something he'd be part of if he and Beth weren't on a mission.

In spite of the cool evening, the porch was full and people stood around his mom's dormant garden, now full of Christmas lights and decorations he'd been tricked into displaying a week earlier than usual. His mom had lied, saying she was ready to get the season started.

The hands had gathered some brush and were about to light a bonfire. That would get a lot of the folks outside under a blanket of stars. He glanced up, tipped his hat to the back of his head. Every time he thought of all those pinpricks of twinkling lights, he remembered the night on his blanket with Beth.

"Did you know they were doing this?" she asked, coming up behind him.

"Not a clue. If I had, I would have made them postpone until after the holidays when we'd have information back on their online friends."

"That would have been convenient." She handed him a plate of barbecue. "You should take a breather."

He nodded as he bit into a rib. "Whose idea was it to see that movie this afternoon? My mom's? Did she give you the tickets?"

"Alan did. I can't believe how sneaky they've been. Or how they pulled all this off so quickly. We just told them a few days ago." She sat on the bench, right at home where his mom had watched sunrise after sunrise. "There sure are a lot of people here."

"Next line is…I didn't know there were that many people living around here."

As she laughed a late arrival's headlights lit her brilliant smile. He wanted to bury his hands in her silken hair and feel it drift across his chest. He wanted to kiss her. Kiss her like he had in that small cave. Make her wonder why he didn't kiss her like that every time they saw each other. Come to think of it, why didn't he?

"You know that the informant is probably here. And if they aren't, it will narrow down the list considerably."

That was why. She wasn't hanging around the Rocking B for him. She was there to catch the informant and possibly get her career back on track.

"How do we narrow down the list? What do you need—"

"No. They're here." Beth covered her horror-stricken face with her hands.

Before he could ask what was wrong, she sprung off the bench, replaced her cute behind with his plate. She squeezed his bicep and jerked him to face his parents, who were escorting a couple he didn't know.

"Oh, my gosh!" she squealed with fake excitement. At least fake to him since he'd witnessed the real thing first hand. "I can't believe you did this, Juliet. How did you get my parents here? This is such a surprise. Sweetheart, meet my parents."

Nick swallowed as fast as he could with four disapproving faces approaching. No matter how cheerful Beth tried to sound, fright made her voice quiver. Future in-laws— fake or otherwise—should have made him jumpier than a jack rabbit. He was actually more worried about the barbecue sauce he was about to rub on his shirttail so he could shake hands with Beth's father.

It was soon apparent their disapproving faces were because they'd been caught off guard. Until his mom's phone call, Carroll and Elizabeth Conrad hadn't any clue who Nick Burke was. Beth had never mentioned him, their fake engagement or current living arrangements.

What chance did he have of convincing her to stay, if she hadn't told her parents there was a possibility?

IT WAS CLEAR Carroll and Elizabeth were upset about Beth's surprise engagement to a man they didn't know. Couple that along with the fact their only daughter hadn't told them she was on assignment in West Texas…

Being her gracious self, Juliet whisked Beth's parents back inside before anything could be verbalized.

"They had no clue. Total surprise and contempt."

Nick was right. She wouldn't argue. At least not with him. The looks on her parents' faces had been easy to read. But they'd come. It was finals week at Northwestern, and they'd jumped on a plane to be here anyway. She had to explain. And thank them. Oh, man, they were going to be mad when she admitted it wasn't a real relationship.

But wasn't it?

Nick's hat was in one hand and his other was pushing frustratingly through his teak-streaked hair. And he paced. Three steps one direction, then a pivot and back again. "*Nada*. Nothing. I get it. Completely fake engagements don't need to be mentioned to your parents. Just mine. And the entire Jeff Davis County of friends we have. What the hell was I thinking?"

"Oh, that's totally and completely unfair. You're acting like this is all my fault. Why should I have mentioned our arrangement to my parents? I didn't know about a party. So how was I supposed to know your mother would invite them here? Or that they'd come?"

"You didn't mention me at all. Did you, Beth?"

He was hurt. She heard it in the soft baritone of his voice and saw the pain in his brown eyes. How could she explain that talking to her parents about anything was like starting World War Three? But she had to try. She wanted to.

"Nick, dear," Juliet said through the screen door. "We have another tub of beer iced down in the bunkhouse. Could you bring it in?"

"Sure, Mom."

"Beth, do you mind helping me a minute?"

Before he could take more than a couple of steps, Beth caught his arm. He didn't turn back to her, just inched away, pausing when their hands met then slid apart.

Tears blurred her vision. She'd never meant to hurt him. Her emotions were getting the best of her tonight, tossing her every which way. Worse than a Chicago wind that hit head-on no matter which way you faced.

Under the gruff, stubborn cowboy was a gentle soul.

She loved them both. She wiped the corner of her eyes and ran into the kitchen. Her mother, still wearing a black pants suit and heels, had a frilly apron tied around her waist and was helping Juliet dish up a fresh batch of peach cobbler. She was smiling like she hadn't smiled in years.

It was absurd that her mother would be happy. She wasn't domestic in the least. The news of an engagement—especially to a West Texas cattleman—should have been enough shock to send her in a tizzy. From the looks of things here, it hadn't.

Her mother looked happy. Then it hit her. Beth was happy, too. Not because of a job. She didn't have one. Not because she'd fulfilled her parents' dreams. Far from it. Nick made her happy. They could be practicing defensive moves, falling in the hay, tangled in each other's arms, or captured and being held in the enemy's hellhole. It didn't matter. She was happier than she'd ever been before.

The idea that she loved Nick—as in 100 percent, with all her being, no-turning-back loved him—was so exciting that she giggled. It bubbled right out of her before she could catch it and hold it inside. "Why, Elizabeth Carroll Conrad, you're blushing," her mother said.

"I'm sorry, Mom."

Elizabeth dropped her spoon and wrapped her arms around Beth. "We'll talk about it later. Juliet explained a little. It's good to know you're so happy." With a kiss on her cheek, her mom left her stunned in the middle of the kitchen.

What had happened? Where was the lecture? Her mother had kissed her in a room full of people. Her queenly manner had been replaced by a mom's affection. A real mom. She heard her father's serious conversation in the living room. His booming professor's voice agreed with something the sheriff said. Then Andrea disagreed. Oh, Lord, not a debate.

The crowd slowed passing through the swinging door to the dining room. To give herself a minute, she carefully propped it open so no one would get a smashed nose. The debate carried on with laughter. Her father didn't seem to mind being on the losing side.

"What would you like me to do?" she finally asked Juliet.

"Enjoy yourself, dear. It's your engagement party," Juliet answered with a wink. "They should be getting that bonfire started any minute. And then the boys are going to play some mariachi music. Maybe you can get that son of mine to dance a little."

"I'm not sure Beth remembers how to dance. It's been a while for you, darling. Hasn't it?" her mom asked without sarcasm. "Does Nick dance?"

Both moms carried cobbler and conversation to the dining room, leaving Beth by the sink. She began washing, but stared out the window. Dancing? Yes, she remembered how. It had been a while, but Beth remembered. She nodded, then suddenly felt the need to ask Nick to teach her. Perhaps she should just kiss him and dance the night away…

No, they had something else to do tonight. Find the informant. Her parents' arrival had really thrown her for a loop. She did an about-face and headed to face Nick who should return any minute.

She saw Kate and Cord whispering just outside the porch window. Then Kate darted inside, leaving her husband on the porch. Kate hung back, hiding behind the counter with her back to Beth.

The sound of boots hitting the wooden steps drew her attention to the porch. Cord stood in front of Nick, who had his hands full with a metal tub filled with beer and soda. "Need a hand?"

"I got it." Nick tried to pass, but the Ranger didn't budge.

"Is this for real?" Cord asked.

"Real beer. Real engagement party. Real what's it to ya?" Nick answered.

"I know we've never been buddies, Nick—"

"Buddies? Nope, I don't think that applies to us."

The town had gossiped over the years about Nick not marrying because Kate had married Cord. Juliet had tried to assure her that wasn't the case. According to her, Nick had never met the right woman.

The iced beer must have been heavy and putting unnecessary strain on Nick's cracked ribs. Beth could see the muscles straining in his arms. "Did Kate send you over for the engagement details?"

Kate had done a lot of meddling in his affairs recently. In fact, she was the one who'd sent Beth to the ranch to stay. The look on Cord's face clearly indicated that Kate had sent him. And he knew that Nick knew it.

"We have concerns that an engagement might be taking the undercover thing a bit far."

"For some reason, Kate doesn't feel like she can ask me herself. Right? I get it. She's kept her distance since the shooting and runs off every time someone brings it up." He took a long look around. "She's too scared to face me so she sent her errand boy."

"Watch it, man."

Hold it together, Nick. He seemed fine. He could handle it. Then he shoved the tub at Cord.

"If Kate wants to know why I'm getting married, she can ask me herself."

Kate backed up. So did Beth. It didn't seem as if either man knew they were there. Music from the portable system on the porch came to life with Frankie Valli's "Can't Take My Eyes Off You." She couldn't turn away. She didn't want to listen to the conversation, but couldn't get her feet to move.

Cord looped his fingers through the screen handle and finally pulled it open. "This isn't about Kate. You should know that Beth is on disciplinary leave."

"Do you need to hear me say that my love life isn't your concern, Cord?"

This was it. The truth. Somehow it seemed like the argument was about Kate instead of their engagement. She was so scared the dishes she held were shaking in her hands. She set them on the counter before she could drop them.

Kate looked startled and worried as she turned toward Beth. And, even more apparent, the woman's eyes held pity. She'd seen a lot of pity in Chicago. A whole department of pity. She knew what it looked like and hated it.

Nick shoved his way through the narrow doorway, keeping his face toward the porch. The icy water sloshed over the edge of the tub.

Cord's swearing could have been about dousing his boots and jeans. But his eyes met Beth's and she could tell he knew she'd overheard the entire exchange.

Nick laughed, his back still to the two women. "Do you really think that matters? Everyone's going to know I have a DEA agent living here. Maybe that will do the job you can't and keep some of the smugglers off my land."

LOOKING AT THE corral there'd been nothing. Maybe a twinge, but nothing major. He hadn't come close to almost passing out. Good. About damn time. He felt strong, even with his muscles aching from the heavy tub. He set it in the corner, pulled a bottle and twisted the cap.

"Maybe you're afraid to let Kate talk to me. Maybe you know she still has a thing for me."

"Are you drunk?" Cord asked, taking an aggressive step inside.

"Uh, no, but I could be soon." Nick laughed and tipped the bottle.

Maybe getting drunk was a good idea. Hell, he didn't know what he was thinking or saying. He knew there'd never be a possibility of him and Kate getting together. There never had been a possibility. Cord's wife was only a friend. She'd always been a friend, since they were children and he'd first moved here. He could see their relationship clearly, especially now that Beth was in his life.

But old habits died hard and pushing the Texas Ranger's buttons was something he'd been doing for quite some time. It was hard to stop and too much fun getting under the other man's skin. Until he saw the look on Cord's face and heard the footsteps behind him.

Beth.

She ran past him, her purple rhinestone boots sliding across the water he'd sloshed on the floor. She slammed through the screen, her footsteps hurrying down the steps. Yelling he could deal with, but not tears.

"Great. Just great." He followed Cord's dumb stare and shrug. Kate's hand was over her open mouth. "Damn it, girl. You haven't said two words to me in the past year, but you sure have a habit of messing up my life."

"We're concerned about you—"

Nick was half way across the porch and didn't wait for her to finish. The relationship he had with Cord would remain shaky. Tonight he'd gone too far because he was upset about Beth. Plain and simple, he was angry he hadn't ranked a conversation with her parents.

He'd wanted Cord to take a swing at him, cracked ribs and all. He'd wanted to take out his aggression on a man who expected anger and smart remarks, instead of facing an honest conversation with the woman he loved. Yes, loved. Completely. Right down to the rhinestones on her purple-booted foot model's feet.

Now he just had to find her and tell her. If she'd forgive him.

Chapter Twenty

Fake engagement. Fake engagement. It's only a fake engagement. Beth repeated the words all the way to the barn. She swiped at the tears, ruining her eye makeup. She'd hang with her favorite horse, Applewine, a little, calm down a lot and sneak back into her room to repair her makeup before she was missed and anyone could wonder what had happened to her.

A fake engagement, she chanted. Why had she agreed to such a thing? And now she had to explain everything to her parents. *Oh, no...her parents!* How long were they staying and were they staying here at the ranch? That would mean she and Nick would need to share a room. Shoot. He could move to the bunkhouse—or she would. There was no way she was sleeping with him again. *Sleeping* would not be the problem. The explosive way she reacted to his nearness was definitely the problem.

Nothing between them had been real. Their relationship had begun with hot, sexy banter...and a night under the stars. It had been a hell of a ride, full of intense situations. How could she have let herself fall for someone so completely different and so completely out of her realm of reality?

So many differences...

Stubborn… He was definitely stubborn, but then, so was she.

He hated her shoes. Even her boots. The man clearly didn't have any fashion sense. And yet that didn't seem to be a bad thing, either.

Horses. He loved his animals and…so did she. She stood at the stall and finger-combed Applewine's mane.

These weren't really differences any longer.

Chicago versus West Texas. How could that one be resolved? Well, she didn't have a job in Chicago any longer. Not really.

But Cord was wrong. The DEA suspension wasn't the reason she'd stuck around. Nick and his family's safety were why she'd accepted the disciplinary leave without a fight. With the exception of trying to find the informant, her time here as an agent had pretty much been a waste. There had been no concrete leads. But then again, she'd accidentally found Bishop. They just needed to pin down his whereabouts and anyone associated with him. Securing him behind bars would give her enough satisfaction while she found another place to work.

Bishop wanted Nick dead and wouldn't stop until he'd achieved that goal. She couldn't have lived with herself if she'd walked away and let that happen.

Greeted by the sounds of the horses, she lifted the latch on the barn door, leaving it open as she walked inside. She needed a good cry. A small pity party for herself. No time for that, but she did need to blow her nose. She sniffled instead, and then scooped a handful of feed from the sack.

Between the stall slats Applewine quickly slobbered up the oats from Beth's hand. The light from the house shone in the doorway and flickered across the stalls. Nick must have followed. Quiet footsteps crunched the hay behind her. His father's classic Sinatra floated in the background mixing with the loud party noises.

Maybe it was time she admitted to him what was bouncing around her heart. Or what was causing the confusing back-and-forth, mixed-up feelings in her head. Because in spite of trying to convince herself otherwise, she was in love with him. He might still care for someone else, but Beth didn't stand a chance if she never told Nick the truth.

"Strange to find you running here of all places," Nick said softly. "A month ago you were petrified of horses."

"Was it only a month?" She stroked Applewine's muzzle, so soft and feathery. She wasn't frightened of the horse any longer, though her ability as a rider was still abysmal.

"I, uh... I guess you heard what I said back there in the kitchen." He shuffled his boots across the dirt, hands in his front pockets. He totally looked the part of a dejected cowboy.

Or a pitiful man who'd been caught doing something silly—no, completely stupid. She couldn't ask him why. Besides having no right to ask—*fake* engagement—she couldn't think of a way to form the question without sounding like a jealous shrew. So, she held her tongue and continued to stroke Applewine's neck, twisting the mare's mane around her fingers.

"For cryin' out loud."

His frustrated tone surprised her, but she kept her gaze on the horse. "Why are you upset with me?" she asked. "I'm not the one who badgered the husband of an old girl-friend."

Okay. There. It was out in the open, jealous shrew and all.

"Kate was never my girlfriend. No matter what anyone thinks or thought." His hands grabbed the top stall rail. His boots were firmly planted as if he was telling the truth.

"That was so abundantly *not* clear in your last conversation with her husband." Yet she wanted to believe him. Both their voices had risen slightly. The horses tossed their heads. Applewine was clearly agitated or maybe the mare wanted another handful of oats. Beth didn't have enough experience to know.

"I was trying to get Cord to…"

"To what?"

"To fight."

"For heaven's sake, why?"

"I was upset after meeting your parents. I know there's no reason I should be. I just needed to knock off some steam and Cord was there. Tonight's been pretty overwhelming."

"If you wanted a bar fight, then why did you follow me?" she asked as she walked to the feed and scooped more into her hand. It had been a little overwhelming for them both.

"I don't want you to be upset."

She fed the mare, then pivoted to face him. "I have never in my life been less upset," she lied. Did he know? The arch of a single eyebrow spoke volumes. Oh, great. He knew.

"You're lying. Just like you did the first day when you said you weren't afraid of the mare I'd brought for you."

"You can't prove it and it shouldn't matter to you. We'll stick to finding the informant. Your parents have dropped the opportunity of a lifetime into our laps. We should be taking advantage of it instead of worrying about what anyone is thinking. You don't owe me any explanation."

"You're right, like always."

"Good, then we should get started by asking your parents if there's someone here they've never met before tonight." She took a step, but he grabbed her shoulders, squaring her with him, nose to nose. God, she loved how tall he was.

"I don't love Kate."

"It doesn't matter to me if you do," she lied again.

"I think it does."

"Why?" she whispered, mirroring the direction of his gaze to her mouth.

"Because I love you."

His firm lips pressed against hers while his hands slid down her arms and around to her back. He pulled her tight against him and she wrapped her arms around his neck, her fingers sliding into the slight curl of hair at the back. Their mouths opened for an onslaught of tingling sensations piercing throughout her body.

Tender, hot, sweet, hard and oh-so sexy. She answered his declaration of love without words. He pulled her closer, crushing her breasts against his hard chest. The need to unbutton his dress shirt and slip out of her sweater had never been higher. But she was responsible and kept her hands around his shoulders.

Nick paused, waiting an inch apart from her. She licked her lips whisper-close to his, making him moan. She should be patient, but she didn't want to be sane. She wanted to be crazy. Throw caution to the wind. Be irresponsible and take exactly what she wanted. She didn't care that a town full of people were on the other side of that barn door. She couldn't resist this man and tugged him back to her. His hands slid under her shirt. His work-rough fingertips danced across her bare skin like a butterfly's wings.

His soft caress, another assault to her senses, turned her legs completely to jelly. Her knees weakened and he pulled back again, arms tight around her, holding her up.

"I think there's something we're supposed to be doing." He bent and kissed the curve of her neck.

"I can't for my life think what it is." She could, but she really didn't want to stop being close to him.

"Something about flushing out the informant and catching a bad guy," he whispered close to her ear, sending tingly vibrations across her lobe. "Of course, that would be your job, not mine. I sort of feel overanalyzed for a while."

"You should have waited to talk to me. I work better when I'm not distracted."

"I found out real quick why men don't like to see women cry. Never bothered me before our escape last week." His voice was low and erotic, mixed with softer kisses he dropped under the edge of her sweater. He drew back, his eyes searching hers. "With everything that's happened to us, to you… I'm sorry I had to ignore your tears in Mexico. I didn't think I could have paid attention to our surroundings. And then—"

She placed a finger over his lips. "Shh. To be honest, I've never cried in front of a guy before. Maybe Danny Bryant in the third grade, but never anyone your age."

"Is that supposed to make me feel better?"

"Maybe not, but it should make you feel special." She drew her own circles just under his slightly scruffy jaw. "I don't know why or how it happened, but I love you, too."

They kissed again. She'd thought the kiss when they'd been captured had been superspecial, but it didn't compare.

Nick shoved his fingers through her loose hair. "Pure silk."

Whatever decisions needed to be made, they would survive.

A knock at the open barn door broke them apart.

"There will be plenty of time for that later, you two," Juliet said from the doorway. "It's time for the bonfire.

All your friends are standing around getting cold while we wait on you to light it."

She left them alone again.

Nick gave her another quick kiss and dropped his hands against his jean-covered thighs with a loud pop. "Guess we should get going."

They passed through the doorway and movement in the field caught her eye. "Do you see that?" She pointed to the dark shadow moving at a fast pace. "Is it a horse?"

"One with a rider. Something's off. I'm saddling the blacks." He squeezed her hand, assuring her it was okay. "Can you find Cord and Pete?"

"Sure, but I should— Nick Burke, you wait on the professionals, do you hear me? Do not take off after whoever is out there on your own. Promise?"

"We're losing time, Beth. Go get the rest of your task force."

He ran inside the barn as she ran to the bonfire. "Morrison! McCrea!" She drew everyone's attention, but the two law enforcement officers weren't there. She finally ran into Alan and gave him instructions. She had to get back to Nick before...

The main barn door flew open and a second later Nick was tearing out across the pasture heading after the man on horseback. She had no idea who it was or if he was armed, but Nick wasn't.

There were no roads in that direction, nothing but a fence for the cattle.

"Great. Just great." To follow Nick she'd have to saddle and ride Applewine. But not without her weapon. She ran into the house, pulled her lockbox from under the bed and grabbed two fully loaded magazines.

"I'll take those." Bishop stuck a gun barrel between her ribs.

She held the magazines up near her ears. Was there more ammunition for her weapon?

"Now the gun."

Would there be another weapon? The gun cabinet had rifles. Alan had pistols in his office. Where was the key? She handed over her gun while mentally cursing Bishop.

"We never considered you foolish enough to set foot on US soil, not to mention the ranch. Are you that crazy? What are you doing here? And why tonight?"

He twisted the gun a little harder. "We're leaving before your *fiancé* realizes he's following the wrong person."

"I'm comfortable where I am. Thanks." She stayed on her knees at the edge of the bed. "You didn't answer my question. Why are you here at the party? It must be something really important considering we had no idea where you'd run off to."

"Get up."

"You want to shoot me? Get rid of us? I'm assuming it's the only reason you'd show up here. So go ahead, but you won't make it out of here alive. There are a lot of ranchers packing out there."

Bishop wrapped his hand in her loose hair and yanked upward. Her hands went to her scalp trying to relieve the pain while she followed his instructions getting to her feet.

"What's your game, Bishop?"

"Hands behind your back." He yanked harder on her hair. "You might not care if you die, but I've got a lot of ammunition to waste on your friends outside. I'd be glad to start with your future in-laws or maybe your own parents."

Beth had to comply. The plastic from cuffs cut into the flesh around her wrists. They were too tight to allow any movement.

"Seriously, what are you planning on doing? Why are you here?"

"The only thing I can do. Eliminate your task force. Let's go. I want to make certain you have a front-row seat."

The bedroom door was almost shut, he shoved her toward it, and she heard a magazine click into place. He draped her heavy coat around her shoulders, successfully hiding her hands behind her back. If she made a sound, he'd begin shooting people, but there was a slim chance she could get someone's attention.

"We're joining everyone else. One word and you know what will happen."

She left her room, turned left to head to the main part of the house and was nudged back to the right instead. Bishop pushed open the master bedroom and she saw that he hadn't come alone. Her parents along with Nick's parents were being held at gunpoint by one of his men.

"There's no reason to hurt anyone else. I'm cooperating," she said.

"And now, you know the consequences if you don't."

Chapter Twenty-One

Nick galloped across his pasture with nothing but a waning moon to guide him. He was chasing after a mysterious horseman without a weapon. The only thing he had with him was his rope.

And if there was one thing a rancher knew how to do, it was to drive a stubborn cow. This cow just happened to be a human whose butt would hurt when it hit the ground. Roping this runaway was faster than catching up to him. Safer, too since he didn't know if the man had a weapon.

He loosened his rope cinch and built a loop securing it under his arm. Kicking up his horse to a faster gallop he lined up and started to overcome the rider. Just a bit closer and he circled the rope over his head to open it and get the velocity he needed to throw. Then he let the rope fly.

Target acquired, he wrapped the rope around his saddle horn. By the time he'd created a dally, his well-trained horse had thrown on the brakes, sliding to a stop before the other horse hit the end of the rope.

Nick hit the ground before his target flew over the rump of his own horse and landed with a hard thud on the ground. The horse kept running, probably scared straight into the next county. The man's straw hat flew away as his moans grew louder from the winter-cold ground. Taking advantage of his target's momentary confusion and change of direction, Nick cautiously approached with no knife, no rifle and only the rope for his defense.

"I can't say I'm sorry. You were trespassing and you'll be lucky if the next place that butt lands isn't in jail."

He yanked hard on the rope, pulling the slack, keeping it taut and low around the man's waist, which trapped his arms. He didn't squirm or try to get free, allowing Nick to get closer. He gave a tug with both hands and the man fell backward. Nick placed his boot on the man's chest but quickly pulled it back.

"Matt? Matt Long?" This was the informant? The kid couldn't even shave.

"Please don't send me to jail, Mr. Burke. Momma said I had to do this or we were all going to get hurt bad."

While the kid continued to plead for his freedom, Nick lifted the loop over his head and pulled him up by his coat lapels.

"Who's going to hurt you or your mom?"

"I...um..."

He'd known this kid his entire life. Had watched him at the local rodeos bronco busting. He couldn't be more than fifteen. That seemed about right, 'cause he'd just started driving around town. His dirtbag of a father had taken off last year sometime after the shooting, leaving the family strapped.

"You want your freedom, kid? You come clean with what you know."

"I heard her talking to somebody a couple of times. Telling him things. I think it's the same guy, but I don't know who he is. Honest, Mr. Burke, honest." Matt's body literally shook under Nick's hold.

"Did she mention when I'd be gone from the ranch?"

"Yes, sir. At least I think she was talkin' about you."

Matt's mother was the informant. Maybe his dad had

been before that. The timing fit, since he'd taken off right after everything hit the fan last year.

Nick released him, patting both the kid's shoulders. "Go get your hat and run home."

"That mean you won't press charges, sir?"

Nick ran his hand through his hair, trying to think. "Why?"

"I'd be willing to work—"

"No. Why did they send you out here?"

Dirt popped up behind the kid's shoulder. Then an unmistakable sound echoed through the cool air.

"Was that a rifle?" Matt asked.

"Let's get the hell out of here!"

He pulled the kid's coat again. First running, then yanking him behind him, barely waiting for him to get his leg over the rear end of the horse before shouting, "Haw!" He slapped the reins and the horse jumped forward. Matt's hands wrapped around him, holding tight.

Beth is at the ranch. With that thought ringing in his head, he kicked the horse's sides harder.

It was wide-open pasture between them and the barn. To reach safety, they were riding straight into the line of fire.

THE SHOTS STARTLED everyone in the bedroom, even Bishop jumped. People screamed outside. Beth's mother—closest to her in the room—darted forward in the confusion and put her arms around Beth's waist.

They exchanged a quick, concealed look that baffled Beth. Why would— Something was shoved into her hands under her coat.

It was the hard shape of a pocket knife. She could cut through the plastic cuffs when she had an opportunity. Bishop yelled and pushed away her mother, who stumbled back next to her father. Beth secured the knife in her back pocket.

Another shot rang out, this one closer to the house. Outside, there was more screaming, running and shouting with a faint echo of music that still played from the party. Inside, the people she loved watched her for answers. They were silent. No one moved.

Bishop's phone rang, startling everyone in the room again.

"What do you mean you missed?" he screamed into his cell. "One out of the three is not good enough. I need them all dead."

Someone was shot. It couldn't be Nick. He was chasing the mysterious horse and rider. Or could it? Those first shots had sounded like a rifle firing and the last was closer, more like a handgun. *No, no, no.*

"You bastard! Who's shot? Is he okay? Did you kill him this time?" Her eyes blurred with tears, but she couldn't cry. She had to believe Nick was still alive. He'd been shot before. He needed her help. Maybe Pete and Cord were heading to Nick right this minute.

Juliet sat on the bed, twisting her fingers in the corner of her apron. She was worried. Beth would pull herself together because their parents needed her help. They wouldn't survive if Bishop won. She had to fight Bishop and defeat him.

"Tie them up and then blow up the tank. Do it." He checked his watch. "You have four minutes."

"Blow it up? You can't hurt all these innocent people." Her mom and dad, Juliet and Alan—they'd all be killed.

"Yes, I can. None of my organization will be bothered by your ineffective task force any longer. Come on."

"You really are a monster."

Bishop yanked her hair again, guiding her through the

doorway, tugging her to a stop at the entrance to the living room. She heard Kate's voice shouting instructions and the sound of dishes breaking. Men's voices she couldn't distinguish spoke all at once.

"Set him down on the island before he bleeds out." Andrea, Pete's girlfriend commanded. "You, dial 9-1-1. Oh, my gosh, he's too tall. Someone will have to hold his feet."

Nick was tall. Then again, all three men on the task force would be too tall for Juliet's kitchen island.

The shouting continued. People ran through the living room, crouching behind furniture. She heard Cord's voice outside, "Get to cover! If you can, get a ride to town. Fast!"

"Move. Front door," Bishop told her softly. He kept her close with one hand twisted in her hair and the other twisting her flesh with his handgun into her side once more.

The front door was open. He pulled on the small hairs at the base of her scalp, causing her to draw air through her teeth. He turned her to the left on the porch, facing away from the barn. The Burkes' friends gave her curious or maybe concerned looks as she headed upstream from those attempting to get to safety.

What was about to explode? *Run!* she wanted to scream at the people to get them out of there before they became victims of this senseless violence. Cord was nowhere in sight. She didn't recognize anyone who passed to silently plead for help. Bishop turned closer into her coat, hiding his face.

Some DEA agent you are. She couldn't stop thinking about her shortcomings or straining to hear voices that would let her know who was bleeding from a gunshot wound in the kitchen. If she'd been a better agent, perhaps this could have been prevented.

Bishop and his men infiltrating the party hadn't ever occurred to her. She had to stop beating herself up over this, over the shooting in Chicago. Some events couldn't be foreseen. But they could be dealt with.

An explosion splitting the night left her ears ringing. The house shook beneath her feet. The blast felt like an earthquake, ten times worse than the car blast when they had escaped. Their four minutes were up.

Bishop laughed and pulled her into the multitude of people now running for their cars. He shot his gun into the air, causing even more panic and ear-piercing screams. His men had successfully blown up the propane tank. Everything was on fire east of the house. The flames would spread quickly into the fields unless someone acted fast.

Options for her freedom, and the four captives in the bedroom, were limited if she couldn't find help. Bishop marched her straight into the barn, shut the main doors and left them in the dark.

A murdering drug dealer stood between her and the only way out. If she made a move, she'd be dead before disarming him. And disarming him with her hands behind her back was too much to expect.

If she could get her hands free, there was a hook they used for the hay on the wall, but the odds weren't in her favor she'd reach it in time. All too quickly, her wrists were not only secured together, they were tied a second time to a rail in an empty stall.

"That should keep you." None too gently, Bishop yanked the rope tighter.

She held in the hiss of pain and ground her teeth, refusing to let him see her flinch. Her wrists were already raw from pulling against the plastic restraints.

"I need you for bait or you already would be dead, *chica*. Keeping you alive is covering our bases, as you say here in America. I will be back to finish you soon. Don't worry."

Bishop tapped her cheek lightly and left by the far entrance.

All she needed was enough time to retrieve the knife from her back pocket and cut through the restraints. All she needed was time.

Chapter Twenty-Two

Nick and his passenger felt the ground tremor from the explosion when his horse stumbled a bit under them. As dangerous as it was, the resulting fire was probably the only thing that had saved their lives from the sniper.

Nick headed to the east, putting the fire between them and the house, then circling the back side. He dropped off Matt close to the drive to the main road and told him to flag down a car for a ride.

He left his horse a couple of hundred yards from the house. His cell finally had reception again, but no one answered. He figured Cord and Pete would be busy helping with the crowd or fire. Then he heard more shots bounce off the buildings. He was unable to determine where they were coming from.

Could he really go back into a situation that might put another bullet in him? Could he risk getting to the spot where he'd been shot and then losing control—staring into space while others were injured? His chest hadn't had the phantom pain since Beth had stroked the scar with her tender touch. He took a deep breath. He pictured the corral, strained to see it on the far side of the garden. No dizziness.

The question was no longer *if* he could go back to his home. Just *how*.

What was Bishop trying to accomplish?

The closer he got, the more his home looked like a mini war zone. No one worked to extinguish the fire. The wind was taking the flames away from the house and into the pasture. He watched men hunkered down behind tool implements instead of grabbing a shovel or water.

Damn, the shots. Bishop's men had folks pinned where they were. He needed his rifle, and needed to find out why Cord and Pete and even Beth weren't stopping the gunmen.

Weaving and staying low to the ground, he quickly made his way to his mother's garden. Praying that his parents had left with someone else, he finally got to the back porch. And a trail of blood.

He took the steps two at a time. His heart exploding out of his chest at the thought it might be Beth bleeding inside.

"You're going to the hospital," Pete's new girlfriend, Andrea insisted. "I've stopped the bleeding, but you were seriously shot."

"I need to find Cord."

Nick yanked open the door, blocking out everything except the picture of Pete sitting where his mom rolled out her biscuits. Shirtless, his arm in a sling and enough gauze stuck to his shoulder to plug a dam.

"You're not Beth." He relaxed for a split second, realizing she was still unaccounted for as he searched faces in the room.

"Nick," the room seemed to say at once. Several people already huddled along the cabinets, out of the way.

Pete swung his legs over the side and sat. "I'm fine. I haven't seen her since before this all started."

"I can't get her on her phone. None of you would answer." Nick felt his own blood pumping again. Everything had completely stopped when he'd thought Beth might be bleeding and dying. She still wasn't accounted for, but she might have gotten their parents to safety.

"We've been a little busy." Andrea crossed her arms. "She might have gotten to a car and might not have her cell."

"No way. She runs to the action. Not from it." His gut was telling him she was in trouble. He had to find her before Bishop did.

Kate looked at her phone. "Cord's still not answering, but I didn't think he'd stop to take my call. It's only been a few minutes since the last shots."

"There are a lot of people pinned down out there." Nick hoped Beth wasn't one of them. "He's got his hands full."

"More reason for me to put on a shirt," Pete complained.

Watching the expression and determination on his girl-friend's face, Pete was fighting a losing battle.

Nick needed to get outside and help. "Did anyone see my parents leave? Their car's blocked in by a couple of others." He searched the faces of people huddled out of the way or helping with Pete's wound. They all shook their heads. Then everyone heard the next shot, turning their faces toward the window just before the cracked pane shattered.

"Down!" Pete shouted. "Lights."

Nick was closest to the door and flipped the switch. The remaining light over the stove shone brightly on the far wall. A single bulb that seemed to keep everyone calm.

"Where's your sidearm?" he asked Pete.

"This was a party. I left it in my truck." The sheriff stood, almost falling before doubling over the kitchen island, silently admitting that he was out of the game.

"No one's come through here in a while," said one of his dad's friends, who sat next to Nick on the floor. "I was lookin' for your dad when the shootin' started. I did notice your fiancé scootin' out the front door with a city feller right before the explosion."

Beth didn't have any friends here.

"What did this guy look like?"

"I'd say he was nice lookin' with nice city clothes. Sharp pointy shoes, looked like gator or snakeskin maybe. Dark, definitely Hispanic."

Bishop had her.

"Did they say anything?"

"No. Don't think so." He scratched his temple. "I did sort of think it was strange that Miss Beth came from the bedrooms and wasn't worried about the gunshots. They walked straight out the front. I got distracted helping with the sheriff."

"Thanks." He turned to Pete. "Bishop must have Beth. I'm taking dad's shotgun and looking for her. If you hear from Cord, let him know."

"Sure thing. I'll follow just as soon as I can stand up."

Andrea sat next to him shaking her head. "He's lost too much blood."

"Keep him here. Did anyone call for help?" he whispered to Kate.

"Both counties are sending everyone they have, but they're still about ten minutes away." Kate shook her head. "You can't go out there alone."

Keeping his head down, Nick got to his dad's gun cabinet and took the twelve-gauge pump action. He shoved shells into the loading flap and poured the box of extras into his jacket pockets. *Miss Beth came from the bedrooms.* He pumped the slide, moving a shell in place, then crossed the hall, missing the board that squeaked. He slowly turned the knob on his parents' room, expecting something fishy behind the closed door.

Opening it a crack, he saw a shaking gun barrel. He smashed open the door, leveling the shotgun toward one of Bishop's men, who dropped his weapon and raised his hands.

All four of their parents began talking at once. He was right. Beth was a prisoner.

"Where's Bishop?" he asked the man as both the fathers tied him up using neckties. "Come on, man. I know you understand me, so just give it up."

"I don't know," the guy said in perfect English. "But I can call him."

"Is that what he told you to say?"

The young man was trembling, but his nonreply was enough affirmation. Bishop wanted to know when he returned.

"We're coming with you," Carroll Conrad said.

"No, sir, I'm afraid you can't. Beth would never forgive me. And I'm a lot more afraid of that than I am of Bishop or his men." He smiled, trying to reassure them all. He yanked on the neckties, verifying they were secure. "Lock him in the closet, Dad."

He sounded confident talking to their parents, but his insides shook with fear. If it was a runaway horse, he'd know just what to do. But this? He'd find Cord and work with him to find Beth. He'd work smart instead of alone.

After realizing he couldn't live without her, he was petrified about losing her.

BETH'S WRISTS WERE RAW, but she'd kept hold of the pocket knife and had sliced through the first restraint. The knife was sharp enough to cut easily. The delay came from the awkward angle of the second tie around the board. Bishop would return any minute. Her head and her gut told her that.

The fire was on the far side of the house, but the horses could smell the smoke and were uneasy in their stalls. She could hear their chests hitting the stall doors as their snorts and blowing grew louder with a couple of squeals thrown in for good measure. They were warning each other of the impeding danger, but it was a constant reminder to her that she had to escape.

A month ago she wouldn't have known any sounds a horse made. Or how scared they became when separated from their herd. Now she totally understood. But she was on her own. She dropped the angle of her hands to a more comfortable position and adjusted her sweaty grip before losing the knife to the ground. She jabbed her hand once or twice as she sawed. Then, one good jerk and…she was free.

Perfect timing. At least for Bishop. Half a minute more and she would have had time to get out into the paddock. She barely had enough warning of his return to get her hands behind her back.

"I am ready to leave," Bishop said into his cell. "When he tries to rescue the senior citizens in the bedroom, one clean shot and my problem is solved." He pointed the gun at her and imitated firing it. "He knows I have his woman. If he survives my man at the house, I guarantee he'll be here soon for me to finish things."

Bishop stowed the cell in his pocket and leaned against a post. Her eyes had grown accustomed to the dark and she could see his maniacal expressions fairly clearly.

"This entire plan was suicide. Why come here with no way out?" She kept her hands holding the top of the rail, giving her the appearance of still being secured.

"You are the one with no escape, *chica*."

One of the horses was getting overly anxious and kicked at the back of his stall. It was enough of a distraction for Beth to jump to the stall door. Bishop swung around holding the handgun at her abdomen.

"Since you are in such a hurry, I see no reason to wait." He raised the gun but a blur crashed down on his arm and soured the kill shot.

"Run!" Nick shouted, tackling Bishop to the barn floor.

Some of their self-defense lessons were paying off. Nick jabbed, braced for a punch to his cracked ribs, swung an uppercut and then rolled Bishop end over end to the other side of the barn.

Beth looked for the weapon Nick had knocked away from Bishop. Nothing. Or if she could reach the hook behind her...

"Beth, run!"

Bishop came up from the floor with her weapon now in his hand. But Nick wasn't finished. He attacked again with a loud growl, tackling Bishop and ramming him into Applewine's stall door.

They wrestled for the gun firmly in Bishop's grip, a familiar struggle. One she'd witnessed in Chicago where she'd hesitated and an agent had died. That was different. She'd been unsure, faced with impossible circumstances of who was who. Here there was no question. Running for safety wasn't an option. She searched the edge of the breezeway for the second gun.

"No!" Nick yelled.

Beth whipped her head around, once again facing a gun. Bishop fired. Nick lunged. Beth dove.

The shot went high into the loft. She rolled to her feet, toward the man she loved and who had become her partner. She didn't need a weapon. She had her fists and could help subdue Bishop.

Nick released him long enough to throw his elbow into Bishop's chin. The gun, still in Bishop's hand lowered between them.

Beth couldn't move or breathe. Neither did either man.

A split second of the universe coming to a halt then her instincts kicked in.

A step away. Hand extended. Another shot.

The struggle ended. She could see Nick's confused expression. One of them had taken a bullet. Then they both slumped to the ground. No!

"Nick!" She stumbled the remaining step to him, holding her screams inside before rolling him off Bishop.

The love of her life was covered in blood.

"It's not me. It's not me." He tossed the gun, then held up his hands, grabbing her shoulders. He shook her until she locked eyes with him.

"You cut that one a little close," she whispered through tears, then pulled his face to hers and kissed him briefly. "Let's try not to do that again for a while."

Beth didn't want to let him go but did as he wearily got to his feet. She placed her hands over Bishop's wound.

Nick found the lights and tossed the first-aid kit at her knees. "I suppose you want to keep him alive for questioning."

She didn't want to think about more questions or smugglers or other impossible plans. She wanted Nick. But they ripped open bandages and applied them to the abdominal wound. Silently. Both of their hands. Together.

The time to say how proud she was of him would come later. He had more reason than most to walk away and leave Bishop to die, but he didn't. Nick Burke was an exceptional man.

Flashing lights and the sound of a siren filled the barn. They finally had help. Within minutes deputies were there taking over. They cleaned their hands with the water hose outside the barn. She turned toward the house but Nick did an abrupt about-face.

"Uh-uh." He pulled her next to the barn out of sight of

most eyes, protecting her in his arms. "Stay here a minute with me. Our parents are safe. We can let the cavalry handle rounding up the rest of Bishop's men."

Exhausted, they propped themselves against the outside wall, letting the rest of the world catch up to their dizzying moment. No words were necessary for once. Just the strong pair of arms around her to make her feel safe, secure and more than a little loved.

Chapter Twenty-Three

The fire was out. They'd be without central heating until they could get another propane tank. Good thing they had fireplaces in the house. Nick took a final look around. They'd lost a storage shed and fencing, but all the animals were safe. Not to mention the people.

Dawn would be breaking soon and he had a full day ahead getting the ranch back into working order. He spotted Beth with Cord on the porch and hightailed it to her side. Not caring at all that he stunk or was covered in soot. He needed to touch the woman he loved.

"Pete's sleeping it off now, but Bishop didn't make it." Cord adjusted his hat. "His men, however, are singing—"

"Like canaries. That's great," Beth finished. She tossed her hair over her shoulder, but the breeze made keeping it there impossible.

"I was going to say mockingbirds. It's more Texan." Cord winked.

"Watch it, now. That's my girl." Nick joined them, leaping up the steps. He was genuinely happy. Glad it was over. Thankful everyone was okay. Grateful he could look at the corral and not freeze. He wrapped his arm around Beth's waist and she weaved her fingers through his. He was definitely used to her being around.

"Hopefully this is the break your task force needs to

find out who's behind all this," Beth told Cord. "There has to be more to it."

"There always is. And you mean *our* task force," Cord corrected. "I'm not letting you off the hook."

"Wasn't it just last night you were trying to warn Nick about me?" She squeezed his hand, keeping him close.

"I didn't have all the facts then. You'll forgive me?" he asked. "I wanted to let you know we're picking up Mrs. Long. Even though odds are she didn't know who she was passing the info to."

Beth nodded. "Will there be a joint effort to gather the rest of Bishop's men in Mexico? Did you assume all along that Bishop was taking orders from someone else?"

"One of the cartels, old or new. You know, there's a lesson I learned a few years back. If you take out the trash, sooner or later, there's going to be more to pick up. We cleared this rabble and sooner—rather than later—we'll have to clear it again. Might even arrest the same underlings."

"But—"

"Beth, how about you take the rest of today off?" Nick stuck out his free hand to Cord. "I owe you an apology."

"We're good."

And Nick knew they were. They'd been set up as opponents by their small community, but not any longer. Now they were all on the same team. "Just the same, I'm sorry for last night. I'm also sorry that Beth can't come to work for a few days. That is, if she decides to go back. Her folks are hanging around through the holidays."

She looked at him sweetly, but in her eyes he could tell she thought he was crazy. He had his fingers crossed she'd agree to a New Year's wedding.

"Come on." Nick pulled her toward the bunkhouse. He

reached through the door and drew back his hand with a set of keys to the Wrangler.

SNATCHING THE KEYS from his hand, Beth ran ahead of him and slid into the driver's seat of her favorite vehicle. She knew where to go without a word. His hill—where he could see his land—even if there would always be challenges. She parked, pointing the Jeep toward the sun that was just peeking over the horizon.

They stood on the seats. Leaning on the roll bar, he gently pulled on her hand and guided her into his arms. The sun's oranges and pinks stretched across the sky, pushing away the dark night. She'd leave the symbolism for later, too. All she wanted was the moment.

Still surrounded by family and friends, there'd be time to sort through all the details later. Time enough to fill out reports and give statements at the courthouse and to the DEA. Right now, everyone was safe and she was wrapped in the arms of her one and only.

"Will you marry me for real, Beth?"

"Maybe." She teased him, remembering what he'd put her through on this very hill what seemed like ages ago. Repeating the words he'd used, "I'd ask me real nice-like. Bended knee, the whole shebang. Then I might consider it."

"Should I wait? Kneeling right now might be a bit of a problem."

"Well, you know your mother's probably showing my mother how to look through the telescope."

"More than likely she's teaching her how to make biscuits."

They laughed. Their relationship had been anything except traditional. So for everyone who may be watching, she gave an answer that couldn't be misunderstood. A very passionate, sexy kiss.

She was comforted by the strength of his body and excited by the desire just his mouth against hers created. Their lips tangled and his hands locked around her waist, keeping her close.

"No more fake engagement?" she asked when their lips parted.

"Nope. And not a long one, either. I'm not taking any chances of you running back to an easier life in Chicago."

"There's really not anything there for me except my parents." Who had been much more accepting of the fake party and invasion than she'd thought they would be.

"Oh, I don't know." He tugged on the pant leg of her jeans, exposing her purple rhinestone boots. "I think you can still make it as a foot model."

"I'd rather just be a simple cattleman's wife," she said, winking. "Of course, there will never be anything simple about living in this country."

He kissed her again. "Deal, 'cause I love you enough to give you what you want."

"Same here."

This hill was now their spot to talk about the future and to watch a lifetime of sunsets and sunrises.

* * * * *

Don't miss the next book in Angi Morgan's miniseries,
WEST TEXAS WATCHMEN,
when THE RANGER goes on sale in March.
You'll find it wherever
Harlequin Intrigue books are sold!

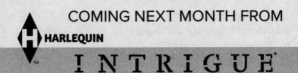

REQUEST YOUR FREE BOOKS!
2 FREE NOVELS PLUS 2 FREE GIFTS!

H HARLEQUIN®

INTRIGUE®

BREATHTAKING ROMANTIC SUSPENSE

YES! Please send me 2 FREE Harlequin Intrigue® novels and my 2 FREE gifts (gifts are worth about $10). After receiving them, if I don't wish to receive any more books, I can return the shipping statement marked "cancel." If I don't cancel, I will receive 6 brand-new novels every month and be billed just $4.74 per book in the U.S. or $5.24 per book in Canada. That's a savings of at least 14% off the cover price! It's quite a bargain! Shipping and handling is just 50¢ per book in the U.S. and 75¢ per book in Canada.* I understand that accepting the 2 free books and gifts places me under no obligation to buy anything. I can always return a shipment and cancel at any time. Even if I never buy another book, the two free books and gifts are mine to keep forever.

182/382 HDN F42N

Name	(PLEASE PRINT)

Address	Apt. #

City	State/Prov.	Zip/Postal Code

Signature (if under 18, a parent or guardian must sign)

Mail to the **Harlequin® Reader Service:**
IN U.S.A.: P.O. Box 1867, Buffalo, NY 14240-1867
IN CANADA: P.O. Box 609, Fort Erie, Ontario L2A 5X3
**Are you a subscriber to Harlequin Intrigue books
and want to receive the larger-print edition?
Call 1-800-873-8635 or visit www.ReaderService.com.**

* Terms and prices subject to change without notice. Prices do not include applicable taxes. Sales tax applicable in N.Y. Canadian residents will be charged applicable taxes. Offer not valid in Quebec. This offer is limited to one order per household. Not valid for current subscribers to Harlequin Intrigue books. All orders subject to credit approval. Credit or debit balances in a customer's account(s) may be offset by any other outstanding balance owed by or to the customer. Please allow 4 to 6 weeks for delivery. Offer available while quantities last.

Your Privacy—The Harlequin® Reader Service is committed to protecting your privacy. Our Privacy Policy is available online at www.ReaderService.com or upon request from the Harlequin Reader Service.

We make a portion of our mailing list available to reputable third parties that offer products we believe may interest you. If you prefer that we not exchange your name with third parties, or if you wish to clarify or modify your communication preferences, please visit us at www.ReaderService.com/consumerchoice or write to us at Harlequin Reader Service Preference Service, P.O. Box 9062, Buffalo, NY 14269. Include your complete name and address.

HI13R

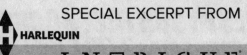
*A Texas deputy steps in to protect a vulnerable witness,
even though she could send his own father to jail...*

"You know that I'm staying here with you tonight, right,"
Colt said when he pulled to a stop in front of her house.

Elise was certain that wasn't a question, and she wanted
to insist his babysitting her wasn't necessary.

But she was afraid that it was.

Because someone wanted her dead. Had even sent
someone to end her life. And that someone had nearly
succeeded.

She'd hoped the bone-deep exhaustion would tamp
down the fear. It didn't. She was feeling both fear and
fatigue, and that wasn't a good mix.

Nor was having Colt around.

However, the alternative was her being alone in her
house that was miles from town or her nearest neighbor.
And for just the rest of the night, she wasn't ready for
the alone part. In the morning though, she would have to
do something to remedy it. Something that didn't include
Colt and her under the same roof.

For now though, that was exactly what was about to
happen.

They got out of his truck, the sleet still spitting at them,
and the air so bitterly cold that it burned her lungs with
each breath she took. Elise's hands were still shaking,
and when she tried to unlock the front door of her house,
she dropped the gob of keys, the metal sound clattering

onto the weathered wood porch. Colt reached for them at the same time she did, and their heads ended up colliding.

Right on her stitches.

The pain shot through her, and even though Elise tried to choke back the groan, she didn't quite succeed.

"Sorry." Colt cursed and snatched the keys from her to unlock the door. He definitely wasn't shaking.

"Wait here," he ordered the moment they stepped into the living room. He shut the door, gave her a stay-put warning glance and drew his gun before he started looking around.

Only then did Elise realize that someone—another hit man maybe—could be already hiding inside. Waiting to kill her.

Sweet heaven.

When was this going to end?

As the threats to Elise Nichols escalate, so does the tension between her and sexy cowboy Colt McKinnon!

Don't miss their heart-stopping story when
THE DEPUTY'S REDEMPTION,
part of USA TODAY *bestselling author*
Delores Fossen's SWEETWATER RANCH *miniseries,*
goes on sale in March 2015.

Love the Harlequin book you just read?

Your opinion matters.

Review this book on your favorite
book site, review site, blog or your own
social media properties and share
your opinion with other readers!

Be sure to connect with us at:
Harlequin.com/Newsletters
Facebook.com/HarlequinBooks
Twitter.com/HarlequinBooks

JUST CAN'T GET ENOUGH?

Join our social communities
and talk to us online.

You will have access to the latest
news on upcoming titles and special
promotions, but most importantly,
you can talk to other fans about your
favorite Harlequin reads.

Harlequin.com/Community

 Facebook.com/HarlequinBooks

 Twitter.com/HarlequinBooks

 Pinterest.com/HarlequinBooks

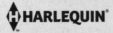